THE FIVE

Earth's Protectors

Dustin Mcclain

This book is a work of fiction. Any references to historical events, real people, or real places are used fictitiously. Other names, characters, places and events are products of the author's imagination and any resemblance to actual events or places or persons, living or dead, is entirely coincidental.

ISBN: 979-8-9939970-2-5 (soft cover)
ISBN: 979-8-9939970-3-2 (eBook)

Dedication

To my wife Susan, who makes everything possible and to my daughter Lucy, you mean everything to me.

Prologue

Charleston, South Carolina
April 11th, 1861

Charleston was thick with the scent of war. For days hushed conversations had broken off when strangers approached, rumors circulating about weapons unlike any seen before–weapons being readied against the Union. William Douglas had caught fragments of these whispers, tales of peculiar foreigners who had arrived to guide the Confederate Army toward independence. Unlike his neighbors, William understood the true significance of these stories. The Deceivers had returned, and it would only be a matter of time before they found him.

William Douglas sat in his study, the fire's warm glow a stark contrast to the thunderstorm raging outside. Lightning flashed brilliant blue, momentarily illuminating the room before plunging it back into firelit darkness. Rain hammered against the windowpanes with such violence it seemed determined to shatter them. Though comfortable enough in Charleston, he knew in his bones he would never truly call this place home. A thunderclap shook the house to its foundation, rattling the glass in its frame. When the tapping came, he nearly dismissed it as more rain until its rhythm registered as deliberate. His eyes lifted from his book to find a face at the window–one he'd never expected to see again. In that instant, he understood he was in grave danger.

William flung open the door and stumbled onto the rain-slick porch where Allan Knight lay sprawled in a widening crimson pool, fingers locked around a gold pocket watch. His chest heaved with uneven breaths, his shirt torn where either bullet or blade had found its mark. When Allan's lips moved, William dropped to his knees, pressing his ear close to catch the whispered words.

"They've found you," Allan rasped, dark blood bubbling at the corner of his mouth. "Run now! There's no time left... nothing can stop what's coming."

With trembling fingers, William gripped his friend's hand.

"Go, my friend," Allan wheezed, his eyes already growing distant. "I'm sorry I failed you."

The final syllable faded as Allan's body went slack. William knelt beside the empty vessel that had once held the only soul who knew his true identity.

Chapter 1

December 1942

On a December evening in the dying year of 1942, under the sickly glow of blackout lamps and the perpetual whine of distant air-raid sirens. By now the United States had spent a full year bled into the Second World War, and the news trailing home from the European and Pacific fronts was gloomy: not only were the Allies failing to gain ground, but the nature of their defeat seemed to shift daily into something more uncanny, more grotesque, as if the world itself were warping around the axis of German ambition. In London, secret rooms buzzed with static and bitterness as clergymen, physicists, and war poets alike tried and failed to make sense of the siege. Paris was a mausoleum; the Soviets retreated through endless snow and frozen bodies. In the Pacific, entire flotillas of American ships vanished, unaccounted for even by the enemy's own broadcasts. Yet it was not merely the scale of defeat that appalled the Allied command, but its flavor–a strange, metallic aftertaste, as if some deeper plot had been laced into history's bloodstream.

For every spectacular defeat, there was a whisper trailing after it: men who did not die by bullet or bayonet but disappeared without a trace, entire battalions reduced to ash as if by the wrath of an Old Testament god. There were rumors that the enemy had developed a type of ordnance that rendered men blind and mute before it killed them, and that certain stretches of the Eastern Front were patrolled by shadowy, silent hunters immune to cold and mechanical failure alike. The Kremlin dismissed these tales as enemy propaganda; the White House, less certain, tasked its brightest minds with cataloging each one. The file grew thick with marvels and atrocities.

At first the Allies pinned their hopes on industry–the relentless multiplication of tanks, planes, ships, and the harvest of steel and flesh from the American Midwest. It was the oldest strategy in the book–what you cannot outwit, you must outproduce. But the new German war engine seemed indifferent to the old equations. They fielded machines that could not be explained by physics, let alone blueprints–aircraft shaped like flattened teardrops painted dull silver like morning stars capable of standing still in midair and then vanishing into the cloud bank without a trace. At sea, U-boats surfaced in American harbors and vanished before a single depth charge could be dropped. There were credible reports of tanks immobilized by invisible hands; convoys lost to silent explosions, and in one case, a platoon of British commandos reduced to gibbering lunatics by exposure to a single, unknown artifact.

There was a name for it, whispered first by the field agents then muttered with increasing desperation by generals and cabinet secretaries alike: Wunderwaffe–wonder weapon. But it was not so much the weapons themselves as the way they seemed to change the very logic of battle, introducing a new terror into the calculus of war, one that Stalin and Roosevelt and Churchill alike were helpless to predict. The best minds of the Allies–Oppenheimer, Turing, Einstein–were set to the task, but even they conceded in coded memoranda and sleepless telegrams that they were losing ground not only in the material, but in the metaphysical. It was as if the Reich had tapped some secret current beneath the surface of reality and was now drawing forth weapons from a future that should never have existed.

Intelligence trickled back to America through desperate missives from the heart of occupied Europe and its fringes, where the resistance had been reduced to whispers and small acts of defiance. Month by month, the flow of information to Allied headquarters dwindled. The weekly deliveries–technical schematics, decoded transmissions, eyewitness accounts from shaking messengers–gave way to an eerie silence broken only by inexplicable reports. The American envoy in Stockholm swore he'd spotted a high-ranking Nazi officer attending "Die Walküre," though newspapers had mourned the man's heroic death at Stalingrad weeks earlier. A British operative received a strange parcel containing nothing but a glossy black stone, mirror-polished, bearing a single etched word: "Rache"–Revenge. It was amid this gathering darkness that the architect of The Five began formulating his plan to confront the Deceivers.

Chapter 2

Bangor, Maine
December 1942

Professor Simon Douglas ran a hand through his wavy black hair, pausing briefly at his slightly receding hairline. At thirty-two, he cut an impressive figure in the hallways of the University of Maine, where students flocked to his physics lectures, not just for his brilliant mind, but for his charismatic teaching style. Though his college football days were behind him, Simon's athletic build still turned heads. What truly set him apart, however, was his unconventional approach to scientific problems, a trait that connected him to his historian father, the Harvard physicist whose classified military work remained shrouded in mystery.

The elder Douglas had earned quite a reputation in the History Department before his retirement. His controversial theories about extraterrestrial influence in ancient Egypt had made him something of a departmental legend. "They've been here all along," he would insist during holiday dinners, eyes gleaming with certainty as he spoke of beings from beyond the stars shaping human events for millennia. Simon's father remained a more distant figure–a Harvard physicist claimed by the Great War before Simon was born. The family knew only fragments: a brilliant academic, a classified military project, a fatal accident. Whatever breakthrough the elder Douglas had been pursuing died with him, sealed away in government archives that no one in the family had ever been permitted to access.
Like his father, Simon possessed an insatiable intellectual curiosity. He moved effortlessly between scientific inquiry and historical analysis, constantly seeking connections between past events and present understanding. Questions others deemed unanswerable became his specialty. Though reserved in demeanor, his determination was unmistakable–whether in academic pursuits or on the athletic field, Simon rarely settled for mediocrity. Teaching had always been his calling, a perfect outlet for his unconventional thinking. Many dismissed his forward-thinking research as the ramblings of an eccentric, failing to recognize how far ahead of his contemporaries he truly was.

Simon hunched over his mahogany desk in his university office where bookshelves bowed beneath stacks of dog-eared physics journals and historical texts, the collection spanning everything from ancient world civilizations to the latest quantum theories. Yellow lamplight pooled across his final lecture notes for the Christmas break, casting long shadows across the worn floorboards. At thirty-two, he was the youngest professor in Maine's science department–a wunderkind whose brilliant theories earned him a coveted position immediately after graduation. The football trophy gathering dust on his windowsill served as a bittersweet reminder of the devastating knee injury that had crushed his athletic dreams during his freshman year. The same injury that kept him from the battlefields of Europe and the Pacific, where his classmates now fought and died, had inadvertently cemented his future in teaching–or so the universe had led him to believe.

The snow had been falling in thick, relentless curtains since dawn, transforming the campus into a ghostly landscape of white-capped buildings and muffled sounds. Simon's office window was now half-obscured by frost feathering across the glass, the glow from his desk lamp inside created a small island of warmth against the encroaching December darkness. He massaged his stiff neck as he finished preparing for tomorrow's final lecture, his thoughts already drifting to Rebecca's cinnamon-scented kitchen and the soft, milky scent of six-month-old George sleeping in his crib. The main faculty building creaked with emptiness, footprints in the hallway already collecting dust as professors and staff had hurried home to begin their holiday celebrations. Beyond the sheltered campus, war consumed the world–its presence felt even in sleepy Bangor, where military aircraft constantly thundered overhead, their metal bellies laden with soldiers and supplies bound for the European front. Simon's fingers brushed against the worn leather of his book bag as he carefully stacked the dog-eared physics textbooks inside when a sharp, unexpected knock splintered the silence.

Simon's brow furrowed, "who would be calling at this hour?" he thought, fishing the pocket watch from his vest. The timepiece gleamed in the lamplight, its polished gold case worn smooth from generations of handling. A long gold chain dangled from it, ending in an ornate silver key that had long ago lost whatever lock it once opened. On his wedding day, Simon's father had pressed the timepiece into his palm with a trembling hand. "My father entrusted this to me," he'd said, voice thick with emotion, "and now I entrust it to you. Someday, when George is ready, you'll pass it on to him." The weight of generations had settled into Simon's pocket that day, heavier than gold. Another knock–sharper, more insistent–jolted Simon from his reverie. He made a mental note to visit his father tomorrow; the old man had slipped on a patch of black ice last week, leaving his right arm in a plaster cast. Knowing his father's stubborn nature, Simon had no doubt he'd find him hunched over his desk, somehow managing his research one-handed, muttering about the inconvenience. As Simon crossed the creaking floorboards toward the door, he decided he would bring little George along–the baby's gummy smile never failed to brighten his grandfather's weathered face.

Simon quickly opened the door to find a stranger looming in the threshold, his dark overcoat glistening with melting snow that pooled at his feet.

"May I help you?" Simon's voice caught in his throat.

"Mr. Simon Douglas?" The stranger's gravelly voice cut through the silence like a blade. His eyes, unnaturally pale against his wind-burned face bored into Simon's with unsettling intensity. "Professor Douglas," Simon corrected, his pulse quickening. Something about this man's face triggered a half-memory that danced just beyond his grasp.

"I need to speak with you in private." The stranger's voice dropped to a whisper. "It is of the utmost importance." His knuckles whitened around a leather portfolio clutched against his chest.

"I was just leaving." Simon extended his hand, fighting the cold dread spreading through his stomach. "Your name is?"

"Irrelevant," the man snapped, ignoring Simon's outstretched hand. "What matters is that we talk immediately. Time is running out for all of us."

Simon cleared his throat. "As I said, I was just about to head out. Perhaps you could stop by tomorrow and set an appointment with the department secretary? We could talk after the break."

The stranger's face remained impassive, like carved granite beneath the harsh hallway light. He raised one gloved hand–black leather, expensive but worn at the fingertips–cutting through Simon's words with a swift, practiced motion.

The stranger leaned closer, his voice dropping to a sandpaper whisper. "Every second counts now." His gaze darted to the shadows at both ends of the hallway before returning to Simon's face. "These walls have ears. I need somewhere secure." The man's expression remained carved from stone, but his colorless eyes never released

Simon from their grip, like a hawk watching a field mouse. "We can't continue this conversation here."

The man reached into his breast pocket with deliberate slowness, producing a small slip of paper. The cream-colored rectangle trembled slightly between his fingers as he extended it toward Simon. In precise, angular handwriting: "Carpenter Mill 8pm."

The stranger whispered, his breath forming a small cloud in the chilly air, "You must not talk to anyone, and please do not be late." He backed away, his polished shoes leaving wet impressions on the worn floorboards. "I assure you I will explain in detail my reasons for this visit." Without waiting for a response, he turned and vanished down the darkened corridor, his footsteps fading into silence.

Chapter 3

Bangor, Maine
December 1942

Simon was certain he did not want to meet this man again, but something inside him–a nagging curiosity like an itch beneath his skin–made him doubt that feeling. Deep within the recesses of his mind, he knew he would trudge through the fresh-fallen snow to the weathered brick facade of Carpenter Mill at precisely 8pm to hear what this stranger had to say, although stranger didn't feel like the right word. The man's piercing gray eyes and the slight crook in his nose sparked a flicker of recognition, yet Simon could not place where or if he had ever seen this man before. This thought consumed him as he reached for his gold pocket watch, his fingers freezing mid-motion when he noticed an unusual warmth radiating from his woolen pant pocket. Simon dug into the pocket and extracted the gleaming timepiece, its polished surface catching the amber glow of his desk lamp. The warmth pulsed against his palm–not scalding but pleasantly heated as if the watch had been basking in the summer sun all afternoon instead of resting in the pocket of a university professor on a frigid December day. "Odd," he thought, running his thumb over the intricate engravings on the case, searching for any clue to explain this inexplicable warmth emanating from cold metal.

With reluctance, Simon slid the watch back into his pocket, gathered his leather-bound notebooks and tweed overcoat, and stepped outside into the biting Maine December afternoon. Snowflakes drifted lazily from a steel-gray sky, melting as they landed on his furrowed brow. Though still unsettled by his enigmatic visitor, his thoughts shifted to the welcoming embrace of home–to George's gap-toothed smile and his wife's cinnamon-scented kitchen. Despite the shadow of war hanging over the nation like a funeral shroud, Simon couldn't help but feel that familiar warmth of the holiday season spreading through his chest. It put an extra spring in his step as he navigated the icy sidewalk, looking forward to the twinkling lights, pine-scented wreaths, and precious time with his family–a brief respite from the darkness that seemed to be engulfing the world.

Beef stew and fresh bread filled the kitchen with comforting aromas as he sat with his wife, Rebecca and little George. Several times during dinner he nearly mentioned the strange visitor, but the words wouldn't form properly. How could he explain something he didn't understand himself? And what reasonable excuse could he offer for venturing out at eight o'clock into the worsening blizzard? Instead, he passed the butter and asked about George's day.

The old Carpenter Mill wouldn't be difficult to find, even in this weather. Simon had practically grown up in its shadow with his childhood home just minutes away and his current residence barely ten minutes more. Though the mill wheels had stopped turning when he was just a child, Simon had spent countless summer afternoons catching trout in its pond and splashing through the creek that meandered alongside the weathered structure.

The clock's hands crept toward eight, and Simon's stomach tightened with each passing minute. He drummed his fingers against his thigh, still without a plausible excuse for venturing out on such a night. "I should check on Father before turning in," Simon announced, setting his coffee cup on the side table as the radio crackled between songs. Rebecca glanced up from her knitting, brow furrowed. "Tonight? In this blizzard? Surely it could wait until after your lectures tomorrow." "I've earmarked tomorrow afternoon for Christmas shopping," Simon replied, which wasn't a lie–he'd circled the date in his planner weeks ago. "I'll be quick, darling." He rose, retrieving his coat from the hallway rack. Rebecca gathered their cups with a sigh. "At least wear your heavy scarf. The wind's howling like a banshee." She moved toward the

kitchen. "I'll get George's bath ready while you're gone." Simon wound his scarf around his neck and settled his hat firmly on his head. "Back before you know it." Rebecca's voice carried over the running bathwater. "Give your parents my love. And remind them about Sunday dinner." "Will do," Simon called back, bracing himself as he opened the front door. The winter air struck him with physical force, stealing his breath. He trudged through deepening snow toward the garage, each footstep crunching beneath him. As he slid behind the wheel and coaxed the engine to life with a reluctant growl, Simon shook his head. "Only a madman would venture out on a night like this," he muttered, watching his words form clouds in the frigid air.

What Simon could not yet know was that his life–and the lives of everyone around him–would forever be altered by what awaited him in the shadows of the abandoned mill. The headlights carved twin tunnels through the whirling snowflakes as he pulled onto the property, tires crunching through the pristine blanket of white. The dilapidated structure loomed against the night sky like a forgotten monument, its broken windows gaping like missing teeth in the weathered brick facade. No other vehicle was visible in the swirling maelstrom; no footprints marred the snow-covered ground. Simon's knuckles whitened against the steering wheel as he peered through the windshield, wipers fighting a losing battle against the relentless snowfall that seemed to erase the world beyond his car's meager light.

Simon's heart started to hammer against his ribs. "An abandoned mill in a blizzard–what kind of fool walks willingly into his own murder?" His fingers trembled as he reached for the gearshift, ready to flee this madness, when a figure materialized directly in the headlights' glare. Simon slammed the brakes, a strangled cry caught in his throat. The man stood motionless, snow swirling around him like a spectral aura, his face eerily illuminated from below. No footprints led to where he stood. Nothing but pristine snow surrounded him, as if he'd descended from the sky itself. Recognition clawed at Simon's mind–those eyes boring into him through the windshield belonged to someone he should know, someone important–but the memory remained just beyond his grasp, taunting him. The man glided through the swirling snow to the passenger side of the car and slipped inside, bringing with him a blast of frigid air and the scent of something Simon couldn't quite place–metallic yet ancient, like old coins buried in earth. Snow crystals clung to the stranger's dark woolen coat and melted slowly, glistening under the dim dashboard lights. Simon's fingers tightened around the steering wheel, his knuckles bone white. The pocket watch in his trousers seemed to pulse with warmth against his thigh. Neither man spoke. The only sound was the rhythmic thump of wipers fighting the relentless snowfall and Simon's own heartbeat thundering in his ears. Each passing second stretched into eternity until the stranger's lips finally parted.

"Thank you for meeting me here," he said, that same gravelly voice scraping the silence like a rusted blade. "Can you tell me what I'm doing here?" Simon's voice emerged steadier than he felt, though his mouth had gone desert dry. The heater's warm air suddenly felt insufficient against the chill that had settled in his marrow.

"My name is Thomas Grant," the man said, turning to Simon with eyes that reflected no light.

Chapter 4

Ulm, Germany
December 1942

Thomas Grant hated that he was right. He'd followed every whisper, every rumor, his every instinct driving him straight into the heart of a top-secret Nazi lab carved beneath Ulm's frosted streets. Now, pressed against a steel support beam, he watched the leader of the Deceivers stride across the hangar floor to confer with the base commander. His heart pounded so hard he feared it might betray him. After nearly eighty years on this planet, he'd never been this afraid.

He'd slipped in easily among the civilian laborers–ragged coat, oil-stained cap, hands coated in machine grease. But masks can't hide the truth forever, and the whispered horrors of this place had coalesced into undeniable fact. He pressed his palm to the cold metal and forced himself to breathe. He had made a vow long ago: only as a last resort would he unleash what he carried inside. But that vow burned behind his ribs, and he knew there was no other way. He had to find Simon Douglas.

Finding Simon wouldn't be the hard part. He knew exactly where Douglas was–teaching at a small university in Bangor, Maine, where the snow piled deep and the wind carried secrets across frozen pines. No–the real battle would be telling Simon everything he needed to know, convincing him not just to believe, but to help. People terrified him; he'd spent decades in the shadows. The only time he'd ever truly connected with someone was twenty-five years ago, in what the world calls the First World War. Thomas had never forgiven himself, and each day since he'd vowed to tell William's son the whole truth of what had really happened to his father Willam Douglas.

Time was not on his side; Thomas knew that he had to make his way to Maine and along the way figure out how he would try to tell Simon things that would be hard for him to accept. He turned and left the hangar deep inside Nazi Germany and began his journey to Maine.

The rhythmic motion of the B&M Express allowed Thomas to reflect on the events that had led to this journey, as he gazed through the frost-laced window of the train, his reflection shimmered like a guilty ghost. Nearly six feet tall and impossibly lean, his face was impossible to pin down–every witness recalled him slightly differently. That was why only one photo of him existed: he and William, side by side, the only real friend he'd ever known.

Snowflakes drifted past like silent witnesses to his guilt. What right did he have to pull Simon into this nightmare? Would Simon's fate mirror his grandfather's? Would he hate Thomas once he learned the truth? Each question was a blade twisting in his chest as the train ground through New Hampshire into Maine.

The locomotive let out a tortured groan as it rolled into Bangor station and shuddered to a stop. Thomas clipped his coat tight around his shoulders, tugged his cap low, and stepped into the icy wind. His boots crunched on fresh snow as he headed toward the university–inexorable, unrelenting–toward Simon Douglas, toward the truth, and toward the last hope he dared to trust.

Chapter 5

Bangor, Maine
December 1942

Simon gripped the steering wheel until his knuckles whitened, his mind struggling to process everything Mr. Grant had told him. The information swirled through his thoughts like leaves caught in a whirlwind, seeming more like the plot of a science fiction novel than reality. Yet here he sat, frozen in indecision, unable to drive away or demand more answers.

Aliens aiding the Nazi war machine? Other aliens fighting to save humanity? Simon's breath came in shallow gasps as the car seemed to shrink around him. His rational mind screamed impossibility, yet something in his gut–something primal and undeniable–recognized truth in this stranger's words. It resonated like a tuning fork against his bones.

"Why me?" Simon's voice cracked. "What could any of this possibly have to do with me?" "Mr. Douglas, Thomas leaned closer, his eyes burning with urgency, "humanity stands at the precipice of enslavement. We need you to pull it back, and we're running out of time." Simon slammed his palm against the steering wheel. "I'm a physics professor, not a soldier! Even if I believed this madness–which I don't–how could I possibly know you're not one of them?" "Mr. Douglas, I am afraid you are the only one left who can help us," Thomas said, his voice dropping to a solemn whisper. He reached into his inner pocket and withdrew a small black case, no larger than a cigarette case but thinner, with a glossy obsidian surface that caught the dim light of the car interior. Simon watched, mesmerized, as Thomas's thumb glided across the surface. Suddenly, the case illuminated with an electric blue glow that cast eerie shadows across Thomas' weathered face. The surface transformed into what appeared to be a window into another world–crisp, vibrant colors unlike any photograph Simon had ever encountered. Thomas' fingertip danced across the luminous display, leaving ghostly trails as images flashed and dissolved with each precise movement, like a magician manipulating reality itself.

"Do you recognize this?" Thomas asked, tilting the glowing rectangle toward Simon. The image that materialized sent a chill down Simon's spine–a golden pocket watch with intricate engravings along its circumference, a delicate filigree pattern that spiraled inward toward the center dial. The chain gleamed with an impossible clarity, each link perfectly defined, culminating in a small golden key–identical in every detail to the watch that now seemed to pulse with warmth against Simon's thigh, safely tucked in his pocket. Simon stared at the image. "That looks remarkably like my own pocket watch," he said, his brow furrowing. What could his timepiece possibly have to do with Nazis and alien conspiracies?

"Not just any pocket watch," Thomas said, his voice dropping to a reverent whisper. "Only five were ever created throughout human history. For millennia, just one had been found–until recently." He held the glowing device closer.

Thomas' finger danced across the illuminated surface. Five nearly identical watches appeared in succession, differing only in the trinkets dangling from their chains. One bore a key identical to Simon's. Another displayed a small cross, and yet another a star. "May I see your watch?" Thomas asked, extending his palm. Simon hesitated. "My watch? Whatever for?"

Reluctantly, he withdrew the timepiece from his pocket and nearly dropped it. The gold surface radiated the same peculiar warmth he'd felt that afternoon at the university. Not scorching, but alive somehow, as though the metal itself were breathing. "It's warm, isn't it?" Thomas asked, though his tone suggested he already knew. "Yes," Simon admitted, cradling the watch in his open palm as if seeing it for the first time. "I don't understand why." "Has it done this before?" "Never–" Simon paused, remembering. "Except today, after our meeting at the university." He looked up at Thomas. "What does it mean?" Mr. Grant nodded, his expression softening as the pocket watch began to radiate heat between them. "The watch recognizes me," he said quietly. Simon studied the golden surface, now glowing faintly in the darkness of the car. "So, this warmth means something," he observed. Mr. Grant's eyes met his with sudden gravity. "If it failed to respond, I would already be dead."

"Dead? What do you mean?" Simon asked, confusion wrinkling his brow. How could a watch determine life or death?

"You hold one of five identical watches. These were forged on my home planet over six thousand years ago and brought here by our people five millennia past, when we first arrived on Earth. Originally, they served as communication devices for our first five protectors–and as our sole means of return. They can manipulate time and space, allowing instantaneous travel–but only back to their point of origin. Our earliest guardians carried them to hunt down a threat we call the Deceivers."

"Your home planet? You relocated?" Simon's voice caught. "I'm not following."

Mr. Grant traced a finger over the black, glossy case. "Our sun was dying, plunging our world into an ice age. To survive, our leaders sent five scouts to look for new homes. When they reported back, they'd found Earth–already inhabited but only by primitive cave dwellers. Our code forbids imposing our will on another species, so for centuries we debated. Some argued we should stay and perish; others said we must relocate to save our species. Finally, twenty-five rebels defied the council and came here, determined to thrive even if it meant altering your world."

Simon shook his head. "Why not find an uninhabited planet?"

"It's rare," Mr. Grant said. "Every other world we surveyed hosted intelligent life. Our principles barred us from supplanting native species–except those rebels chose otherwise."

"So, these twenty-five–the Deceivers–arrived against orders?"

"Exactly. We severed their return to our world once we learned of their dark designs, that they intended to dominate humankind. That's why I was sent, with four others, to stop them. I've been here since your Civil War, and I'll remain until I die–our sun went dark not long after I arrived." He glanced out at the swirling snow. "It still reminds me of home."

"You've been here since the Civil War? How old are you?"

Mr. Grant offered a rueful smile. "I age one of your years for every seventy of mine. I was thirty-five by our measure when I came here. I accepted a lifetime on Earth if it meant stopping the Deceivers."

Simon leaned forward. "If your people first came thousands of years ago, why send protectors so late?"

Mr. Grant's eyes grew solemn. "I came with the last team of five."

Simon swallowed. "Where are the others now, and why involve me?"

"They're gone," Mr. Grant said, holding up the second case. A photograph embossed on its surface showed a colossal device–like an oversized spinning top. "This is why you're needed. The Deceivers have nearly activated this weapon. Once operational, it will grant them total dominance over Earth."

Simon stared at the image. "So, you're saying they backed Nazi Germany's rise and helped develop world-conquering weapons?"

Outside, the wind rattled the car, and the snow fell thicker. Simon checked his own watch. "I must go. It's late–my wife will worry and probably already called my parents."

He reached for the ignition, but Mr. Grant's warm hand gently stopped him. "Just a moment longer, Mr. Douglas. You need to hear all of this. Your part in what comes next is crucial."

Simon hesitated, curiosity and dread, warring in his mind, as Mr. Grant began to speak again.

Chapter 6

Cambridge, Massachusetts
January 2001

The cursor blinked accusingly on Jack Douglas's monitor as he scrolled through his inbox, each unopened email another excuse to postpone cracking open his physics textbook. His muscles ached from the afternoon hockey match, the familiar post-game restlessness making academic focus impossible. While his fingers mechanically clicked through messages, his mind replayed the third-period breakaway–the puck sliding just inches wide of the net. A perfectionist's curse. Even as a freshman standout at Harvard, Jack couldn't shake the feeling that every missed shot represented personal failure, regardless of how many he'd managed to score.

Being from a long line of gifted athletes, Jack possessed the kind of natural talent that made coaches salivate. On the ice, his 6'5" frame moved with surprising grace, his powerful legs driving him forward with explosive speed while his broad shoulders allowed him to bulldoze defenders who dared challenge him. Teammates had nicknamed him "The Douglas Express" after watching him barrel down the right wing, unstoppable as a freight train yet precise as a surgeon when releasing his trademark slap shot. In the classroom, Jack's mind worked with similar efficiency, dissecting complex physics equations with the same intuitive understanding that had allowed his father to become the renowned expert on ancient technology used by past civilizations.

Jack had never met his grandfather, Simon Douglas, but the sepia-toned photographs his grandmother kept in her antique cherry wood jewelry box told a story of uncanny resemblance. In those faded images, his grandfather's thick jet-black hair, the same inky shade that Jack saw in his own mirror, swept across a high forehead. The penetrating dark brown eyes that stared back from those photographs seemed to follow Jack across decades, holding the same intensity he recognized in himself. Only the height differentiated them; Jack's towering 6'5" frame outreached his grandfather's respectable 6'1". His grandmother often remarked, with a trembling voice and misty eyes, how they even shared the same purposeful gait–shoulders slightly forward, head tilted at a thoughtful angle. Simon had vanished when Jack's father was merely six months old, his abandoned Chevrolet discovered at the crumbling Stillwater Mill with its driver's door ajar, keys still dangling in the ignition. Jack's father rarely spoke of the man, but Jack's grandmother had never removed her wedding band, as if the gold circle was a tether to the possibility that someday, somehow, Simon Douglas might return to the Victorian house on Highland Avenue where she still left the porch light burning every night.

A sharp knock at the door yanked Jack from his thoughts. His hand instinctively reached for the monitor's power button, the screen going dark just as he called out. "Door's unlocked," he shouted, swiveling in his chair. It was his best friend, Kevin Hall, whose lanky frame and perpetually disheveled sandy hair made him look like he'd just rolled out of bed. They had grown up together in the pine-scented neighborhoods of Bangor, Maine, and both had been accepted to Harvard–Jack on a partial hockey scholarship, Kevin on academic merit despite his casual disdain for authority. Kevin lived in a perpetual haze of caffeine, his fingers tinted orange from energy drink powder and his laptop bag worn diagonally across his torso like military gear. Jack had lost count of the late nights when he'd glance over to find his friend's wire-rimmed glasses illuminated by the blue glow of multiple devices, his eyes still scanning code at 3 a.m.

"Hey hockey star, you want to grab some grub down on Mass Ave? That Thai place with the spring rolls you demolished last week has a student special," Kevin said, leaning against the doorframe with one foot crossed over the other, exposing the worn sole of his sneaker.

"No, I'm good man," Jack replied with a grimace as he stood, a sharp twinge shooting through his bruised ribs where a defenseman's elbow had caught him during the third period. "Already wolfed down a protein shake and sandwich after the game. Think I'll just kick back here and try to decode these quantum equations before my brain turns to mush."

"Fine, be responsible," Kevin sighed dramatically, then brightened. "We still on for Professor 'whack job' tomorrow night? The guy who thinks the burning bush was actually an alien communication device?" He wiggled his fingers in a mock-spooky gesture. Jack unzipped his backpack and yanked out his physics textbook. "I'll be there, but hockey practice runs late. Just save me a seat–not that you'll need to. This guy thinks crop circles are alien landing pads."

Kevin flashed a grin and tapped the door frame twice with his palm. "Their loss. Tomorrow night, then." The door clicked shut behind him, leaving Jack alone with the silence of his dorm room.

Jack glanced at his phone on the nightstand. He should call his dad–their post-game debriefs were practically ritual. The same dad who'd spent countless evenings at the kitchen table, spreading out newspaper clippings about ancient astronaut theories while Jack's mother rolled her eyes good-naturedly. Those conversations had planted seeds that grew into Jack's fascination with unexplained technological leaps throughout history–from impossibly precise pyramid construction to the Third Reich's scientific advancements that seemed to materialize from nowhere.

Unlike his father, Professor George Douglas who was now wrapping up his distinguished career teaching American History at UMaine, Jack couldn't see himself standing before lecture halls. The Douglas academic lineage stretched back generations–from his great-grandfather, the Harvard professor whose brilliant career ended in a classified military accident during WWI, to his grandfather Simon Douglas, whose tenure at UMaine concluded with an unsolved disappearance. Jack tossed his physics textbook aside and stretched across his bed. Research was his calling–diving into primary sources, testing hypotheses, following evidence wherever it led. He had no inkling that his carefully plotted academic path would soon veer wildly off course, carrying him across continents in pursuit of answers about his grandfather's fate and a secret society older than recorded history itself.

Chapter 7

Cambridge, Massachusetts
January 2001

Jack's muscles protested as he rolled out of bed. Yesterday's hockey game had left him battered, and the thought of afternoon practice made him wince. Every bone in his body rebelled against the idea of taking another check into the boards.

He shuffled to his desk and booted up his computer, thinking he might tackle his U.S. History term paper. While the monitor hummed to life, he rotated his neck, wincing at the crackling sounds. A quick email check revealed nothing urgent, just Kevin's reminder about tonight's guest speaker.

His stomach growled. Breakfast first, then class. Jack switched off the monitor, tugged on a rumpled shirt and his favorite worn jeans, slung his backpack over his shoulder, and headed out into the January chill of Massachusetts Avenue. His stomach gnawed at him with a hollow ache that only pancakes stacked three-high and drowning in maple syrup could satisfy–with a side of eggs, sunny-side up, their yolks like small golden suns.

Jack trudged down to Mass Ave, where fresh snow drifted from a pearl-gray sky in fat, lazy flakes that melted instantly on his flushed cheeks. January's bitter teeth bit through his thin Harvard sweatshirt, forcing him to tuck his reddened fingers into his armpits between futile attempts to warm them with his breath. The neon "OPEN 24 HRS" sign buzzed and flickered above Manny's Diner, a cramped establishment where the linoleum floor stuck to the soles of his sneakers and the air hung heavy with the scent of burnt coffee and bacon grease. Jack slid into a window booth with cracked vinyl seats, knowing the food might be mediocre but the portions would be generous.

Across the street, a figure in a steel-gray overcoat stood frozen against the January wind. Thomas Grant clutched the pocket watch chain until his knuckles went white, studying the young man through the diner window. Jack Douglas's profile struck him like a photograph come to life–Simon's jawline, Simon's characteristic tilt of the head. For days, Thomas had shadowed him: from the uppermost rows of the hockey arena where Jack crashed against the boards, through the labyrinthine of campus corridors, cataloging routines, patterns, and vulnerabilities. Nights found Thomas in a hotel room transformed into a shrine of surveillance–photos taped to walls, yellowed newspaper clippings, family histories meticulously charted across generations. His fingers shook as he marked another X on the calendar. The countdown had begun. The Deceivers were moving. At Simon's burial, Thomas had promised never to endanger another Douglas, yet here he stood, about to pull Jack into the same conflict that had buried his grandfather.

Chapter 8

Ulm, Germany
December 1942

Simon Douglas pressed his forehead against the cold glass of the train window, watching skeletal winter trees blur past. His mind remained foggy after the whirlwind of the past few days–alien conspiracies, golden watches with unimaginable power, and the haunting image of his wife's face played repeatedly in his mind... would he ever see her or George again? The rhythmic clacking of steel wheels over track joints provided a hypnotic comfort, while outside, heavy gray clouds hung low, threatening snow just as they had the night he'd abandoned his teaching position and family in Maine.

Four days of travel had passed in near silence. Thomas Grant sat beside him, ramrod straight in his immaculate gray suit, eyes constantly scanning their surroundings, lips barely moving when he spoke. The man was a cipher–offering tantalizing fragments about Deceivers and Protectors, but never the complete picture Simon craved. Each unanswered question twisted Simon's stomach tighter. Could he truly trust this stranger with the piercing blue eyes who claimed Earth's fate hung in the balance?

Simon marveled at the leather document wallet Grant had produced at each checkpoint. With a flick of his wrist and a few murmured German phrases, uniformed men who had been scrutinizing other travelers suddenly snapped to attention, offering curt nods and waving them through. Even now, as their train cut through the heart of the Third Reich–where every railcar should have been requisitioned for moving troops or munitions–they traveled in relative comfort, two inexplicable passengers on a journey toward either salvation or doom.

The train's sudden deceleration jerked Simon from his fitful sleep, his head snapping forward then back against the leather headrest. Through frost-laced windows, he glimpsed a dimly lit platform emerging from the darkness. Gaslights cast yellow halos in the falling snow, illuminating the stark black-and-red banners that hung from the station's façade.

"Come," Mr. Grant whispered, his gloved fingers digging into Simon's forearm. "This is Ulm." His companion's face remained impassive, but his eyes darted continuously, scanning each shadowy corner of the platform where armed sentries stood at attention. "Stay close behind me and speak to no one." They stepped from the heated compartment into the bitter cold of Nazi Germany, their breath forming conspiratorial clouds in the winter air of 1942.

Despite the late hour, the town square bustled with activity. German soldiers in field gray uniforms clustered in small groups, cigarettes glowing like fireflies against the darkness. Civilians hurried past with collars turned up against the cold, their faces drawn with the quiet tension of wartime. As Simon and Mr. Grant moved away from the station, the military presence gradually thinned, leaving only scattered townspeople making their way home through streets muffled by falling snow.

Mr. Grant led them across the cobblestones, now slick with fresh snow, toward a half-timbered building at the far end of the square. The Bavaria House stood three stories tall, its windows glowing amber against the darkness, wisps of chimney smoke curling into the night sky. Simon's eyes traced the ornate Gothic lettering on the wooden sign that swayed gently in the winter breeze. Though he could decipher the German words perfectly in his mind, his tongue felt leaden at the prospect of speaking them aloud. Years of academic study had given him an excellent grasp of vocabulary and grammar, but his Massachusetts accent stubbornly clung to every syllable he attempted, marking him instantly as an American. Throughout their perilous journey, Grant had shielded him from this liability, intercepting every interaction with fluid, native-sounding German that left officials nodding with respect rather than suspicion.

They made it to the entrance of the Inn when Mr. Grant stopped and whispered, "I will take care of this, just listen." They walked inside and Mr. Grant immediately began talking as if he knew the man at the desk, Simon heard Mr. Grant ask about his accommodations and the accommodations of his companion as he motioned toward Simon. The man behind the desk nodded in agreement, turned to the rear wall and retrieved two room keys and handed them over to Mr. Grant. Simon heard the man say, "It's good to have you back Herr Grant; I trust your travels went well?" "They did indeed, thank you Herr Walker," Mr. Grant said as he took the keys from the man.

Mr. Grant turned to Simon; speaking perfect German, he handed him a key and made arrangements to meet him in twenty minutes for a late dinner in the tavern that adjoined the inn. Simon did not speak, only nodded in agreement and then followed Mr. Grant to the stairway leading to the second-floor location of their rooms.

Simon stood at the frost-edged window, watching snowflakes spiral down through pools of gaslight. Each flake seemed to carry his thoughts across the Atlantic–to Elizabeth's worried face, to little George's bedtime prayers going unanswered. Would they think him dead? Deserter? The square below had emptied considerably; only a few soldiers remained, their cigarettes carving brief orange arcs through the darkness as they gestured. A sharp, precise rap at the door broke his reverie. Mr. Grant entered without waiting for an invitation, his leather gloves still on, snowmelt glistening on the shoulders of his immaculate wool coat.

"Mr. Douglas," he whispered, his breath visible even in the heated room, "we must speak now about what our task is to be and what help you are to provide." His blue eyes darted to the window, then the walls, as if enemies might materialize from the wallpaper.

"Come," Grant continued, extending a gloved hand toward two high-backed chairs positioned beneath the leaded glass window. "Let us sit where we can observe the square while I bring you up to date."

Chapter 9

Cambridge, Massachusetts
January 2001

Jack slid into the empty seat beside Kevin, his hair still damp from the locker room shower.

"Look who decided to join the living," Kevin muttered, shifting to make room. "Coach hold you hostage again?"

"Something like that," Jack whispered back, rubbing his sore shoulder. Three rows behind them sat a man in a dark coat–the same figure who'd been watching Jack's apartment that morning–but Jack's attention remained fixed on the podium.

Kevin nodded toward the stage. "You haven't missed the headliner. Just some administrative drone warming up the crowd."

Thomas stared past the podium, his mind elsewhere. The boy shouldn't be dragged into this, yet what choice remained? All signs indicated the Deceivers were emerging from the shadows again. If he hesitated now, the window for action might slam shut forever.

He glanced at his wristwatch–a simple human device, nothing like the artifacts he sought. The world of 2001 barely resembled that of 1942. Humans had accelerated their technological development at a pace that often frustrated Thomas's efforts to stay ahead. Though he and Simon had managed to thwart the Deceivers and help topple the Nazi regime, victory had come at considerable cost. Now the enemy was resurfacing across multiple theaters of operation, and this time, Thomas feared, the battle would prove far more challenging than the last.

Since 1945, Thomas had been hunting the four missing watches, racing against those who would misuse their power. His worst fears were materializing now–someone had found at least one, contributing to this new global threat. The Deceivers had adapted their strategy, becoming more subtle in their conquest. Though created as tools for communication and transportation across vast distances, the watches contained technological secrets that, if fully unlocked, would unleash capabilities this planet had never witnessed. Such power was never meant for Earth–the watches were stranded artifacts from a civilization far beyond human comprehension.

The thunderous applause from the packed auditorium jolted Thomas from his reverie, his weathered hands gripping the armrests as Harrison Carver approached the podium. The man cut an impressive figure–silver-haired, square-jawed, with the confident stride of someone accustomed to skepticism. Thomas had monitored Carver's rise among what the internet age had branded "Conspiracy Theorists," watching as his YouTube videos garnered millions of views and his self-published books climbed obscure bestseller lists. These modern prophets with their PowerPoint presentations and merchandise tables were spreading theories about alien interference in human affairs that made Thomas's neck prickle with unease. Not because they were wrong–quite the opposite.

Beneath Carver's sensationalist claims about ancient astronauts and government cover-ups lay fragments of dangerous truth, pieces of a puzzle that, when assembled, would reveal exactly what Thomas had spent every moment of his time on earth trying to stop. He scanned the rapt faces in the audience, wondering how many more lectures, how many more viral videos, before someone finally connected all the dots.

Harrison Carver's voice filled the auditorium as he described his archaeological expedition to the Mexican jungle. "The evidence was unmistakable," he declared, gesturing emphatically. "Not only have extraterrestrials visited our planet in the distant past, but I believe they walk among us even now."

"So, what'd he dig up? Martian bones? A flying saucer?" Kevin snickered under his breath.

Jack leaned forward in his seat, eyes fixed on the stage. "Shut up," he muttered, elbowing Kevin's ribs. "I want to hear this."

Harrison Carver's voice faded to a distant buzz as the overhead screen illuminated with the image that caught Jack's attention–a gleaming gold pocket watch excavated from Mayan ruins dating back three millennia. The pristine timepiece hung from a long chain, culminating in what appeared to be a cross. Not a single scratch marred its surface; it might have been forged mere hours ago instead of buried for thousands of years.

Thomas's blood turned to ice. His fingers dug into the armrests until his knuckles whitened. There it was–one of the four missing watches he'd hunted across continents and decades. His pulse hammered in his temples as decades of fruitless searching crystallized into this moment of horrifying validation. The artifact that could trigger humanity's extinction was now being paraded before hundreds of oblivious spectators, its image captured on countless phones. If the Deceivers were here–and Thomas knew they must be–the race to claim the watch had just become a desperate sprint toward Armageddon.

Mr. Carver gestured toward the projected image with reverent hands. "Ladies and gentlemen, consider what you're seeing. This timepiece lay entombed beneath centuries of jungle growth and Mayan stonework for over two millennia. Yet when I extracted it from its earthen prison, it required nothing more than a gentle cloth to reveal its unblemished surface." He paused, scanning the audience. "Most remarkable of all–it continues to tick with atomic precision, as if it were crafted yesterday."

Mr. Carver leaned into the microphone, his voice dropping to a near whisper that somehow filled the auditorium. "Consider the environment–centuries of acidic soil, seasonal flooding, root systems penetrating every crevice. Modern electronics fail after a single rainstorm, yet this device survived millennia underground with its mechanism intact." He paused, letting his gaze sweep across the silent crowd.

"The implications are unavoidable. We are looking at technology that predates human capability by thousands of years."

Kevin leaned in close, his breath smelling faintly of the mint gum he'd been chewing throughout the lecture. "I think this guy has been baking his brain in the Mayan sun too long if he thinks anyone with half a neuron is buying this Indiana Jones nonsense," he whispered, rolling his eyes dramatically.

He nudged Jack's arm with an insistent elbow, already half-rising from his squeaky auditorium seat. "Come on man. Let's bail and grab some atomic-hot wings over at Flannery's. Julie's working tonight–you know, the one with the nose ring and the Celtic tattoo?" His eyebrows waggled suggestively. Jack remained transfixed by the golden watch projected on the screen, its perfect surface seeming to glow with an inner light. "No, you go ahead," he murmured, absently shaking his head. "I'll catch up later. I want to hear the rest of this."

"Suit yourself, Professor Strange," Kevin sighed, squeezing past Jack's knees with an exaggerated grimace. He paused in the aisle, backpack slung over one shoulder, and added, "I'll save you a seat before the place gets packed with the post-lecture crowd." Then he slipped out through the exit, the heavy door whooshing shut behind him.

Thomas froze mid-breath when a figure across the auditorium rose from his seat. The silhouette burned into his retinas like a photographic negative–unmistakable even at this distance. The blood in Thomas's veins crystallized as the man slipped toward the exit.

Sixty years evaporated in an instant. That same angular jaw. Those predatory eyes. The architect of the Reich's most devastating weapons stood not fifty yards away, unchanged by the decades that had carved deep lines into Thomas's own face.

A Deceiver.

Here.

Now.

Thomas's fingers clawed into his thighs as memories of burning laboratories and screaming test subjects flooded back. The creature that had once smiled while demonstrating how efficiently his "prototypes" could liquefy human organs was now vanishing through the exit door.

Chapter 10

Ulm, Germany
December 1942

Thomas Grant leaned forward across the small table, his voice low but deliberate. Simon Douglas shifted in his chair, anticipation tightening his chest. At last, he would learn what role he was expected to play in this strange affair–and whether he would accept it. The door to escape hadn't yet closed completely; he could still refuse and somehow find his way home, though the logistics of that seemed impossible. One thing remained certain: he wouldn't commit to anything without full disclosure.

"May I see your watch?" Thomas asked.

Simon's fingers dipped into his pocket, finding the timepiece that had become a familiar presence against his skin. Its peculiar warmth had neither intensified nor diminished since his journey with Mr. Grant began–just a steady, unnatural heat that defied explanation. He extended his palm, offering the golden object. Thomas took it carefully and placed it on the wooden surface between them.

Mr. Grant's eyes darted to the shadows in the corner before he leaned in so close that Simon could smell coffee and fear on his breath. "Do you remember what I told you about this watch?" The words barely escaped his lips.

Simon's throat tightened. "Yes. Communication device. Space-time manipulation for travel."

"It's far more powerful than that." Grant's fingers clenched around the timepiece until his knuckles whitened. "With this watch, we're going to obliterate their plans and end this godforsaken war before they can unleash hell on earth." His voice trembled with urgency as his eyes locked onto Simon's, pupils dilated with terror or madness–perhaps both.

Thomas's voice dropped to a reverent whisper as he revealed the true nature of the five watches to Simon. His weathered fingers traced the intricate engravings on the golden case, lingering on symbols that seemed to shift under Simon's gaze. "These timepieces," Thomas explained, "were forged in the crystalline chambers of our home world and entrusted to the original five Protectors." The watch in his hand suddenly projected a shimmering holographic display that bathed their faces in ethereal blue light. Simon gasped as three-dimensional blueprints of impossible machines rotated before his eyes. "Beyond mere communication and transportation," Thomas continued, "each watch contains vast libraries of technological knowledge–weapons systems that harness dark energy, medical procedures that can regenerate entire limbs, propulsion designs that bend the fabric of space-time." Thomas snapped the watch shut, and the ghostly images vanished. "But their creators were cautious. Only when all five watches are united, their unique chain symbols aligned in sequence, can their full power be unleashed." He leaned forward, his eyes reflecting the golden gleam of the watch. "Without these, the Deceivers are like children fumbling with matches–dangerous but limited. They lack the scientific minds to reverse-engineer what they've merely witnessed, just as you couldn't build an airplane after simply riding in one."

Thomas continued, his voice gaining a reverent quality. "When the first five Protectors were dispatched to Earth in pursuit of the twenty-five Deceivers, each warrior was entrusted with an identical timepiece forged from luminous gold that seemed to capture starlight within its metal. The watches themselves were perfect twins–each with the same intricate celestial engravings along the rim and the same iridescent crystal face that shifted colors depending on the angle of light. The only distinction lay at the end of each gold chain: one bore a miniature silver tree with roots that wrapped around a blood-red ruby; another displayed a perfectly carved falcon with wings outstretched; the third featured a polished obsidian pyramid etched with microscopic symbols; the fourth held a sapphire-encrusted trident; and the fifth–" he patted his own pocket, "–this compass rose of platinum and amber." His expression darkened. "Each Protector received the same grave warning: under no circumstance could these watches fall into Deceiver hands, especially not all five simultaneously. If capture seemed imminent, they were to conceal the watches using an ancient encoding system of glyphs and riddles–a method so complex that only one versed in our world's forgotten language could decipher the trail and return the watches to our dimension."

The Deceivers had anticipated our response with cunning precision. When our world's High Council dispatched the original five warriors through the shimmering quantum portal, the Deceivers were waiting with crystalline detection grids that lit up the night sky. Our warriors materialized on Earth amid a storm of alien weaponry–coruscating beams of violet energy that could disintegrate flesh and bone in seconds. Pursued across continents, from the frost-bitten Siberian tundra to the suffocating heat of the Sahara, our warriors fell one by one. The last of them, bleeding from a wound that leaked silver-blue ichor, managed to conceal four watches beneath ancient monuments, encoding their locations in petroglyphs visible only under the light of specific celestial alignments. When the silence from Earth stretched into months, the Council sent five more warriors, their bodies enhanced with bio-mechanical implants beneath their human disguises. They arrived to find a world already bending to Deceiver influence–one watch had been captured and was generating ripples of temporal distortion around centers of human power. The warriors returned through the portal with haunted eyes and scarred bodies. In the Council's obsidian chamber, illuminated by the glow of a thousand floating data spheres, the final resolution was passed: the Protectors would be formed, an elite corps trained in both our technology and human ways, tasked with recovering the watches while systematically undermining Deceiver operations across the centuries of Earth's vulnerable history.

Simon leaned back in his chair, the wooden legs creaking against the floorboards. "Why didn't you just send an army of your people to hunt them down and destroy all of the Deceivers?" he asked, his fingers drumming nervously on the tabletop.

Mr. Grant's weathered face tightened, deep lines forming around his mouth. "That was our first thought," he said, his voice dropping to a near-whisper. "But humans were already too far advanced by this point. An invasion of that scale would have devastated your cities, your infrastructure." He spread his hands, palms up. "The Deceivers had already interbred with humans for generations. Their genetic alterations are woven into your very DNA now–subtle changes that heightened aggression, encouraged tribal thinking."

The gold watch gleamed on the table between them as Mr. Grant glanced at it, then toward the curtained window where twilight shadows gathered. "We must go now to dinner," he said, rising stiffly. "If we don't show, it will raise suspicion. The walls in this place have ears." Simon tucked the watch carefully into his vest pocket. "We'll continue our talk after." Thomas said as he stood back from the table.

Chapter 11

Cambridge, Massachusetts
January 2001

Thomas eased through the crowd with practiced invisibility. Decades of fieldwork had taught him how to become forgettable–a face that slipped from memory the moment one looked away. He rose silently and drifted toward the hall, pulse quickening. The Deceiver's unexpected presence left him without a strategy. Experience had taught him their habits: they hunted in pairs, sometimes more, never alone. Confrontation now would be suicide, especially with an unknown number lurking nearby. If they identified him–the last Protector–their path to Earth's domination would be unobstructed. Thomas pressed his back against the wall, weighing his limited options. This complication forced his hand. He would need to approach Jack Douglas far earlier than he'd intended–before the boy was ready to hear the truth.

Thomas shadowed the Deceiver through the crowded auditorium, studying the back of the man's perfectly groomed silver hair. He'd known him as Hermann Beck during the Nuremberg trials, but undoubtedly, he'd shed that identity like a snake's skin, assuming a new name with forged credentials that would withstand any human scrutiny. Thomas slipped between clusters of chattering students, his weathered hands kept casually in his pockets, eyes never lingering too long on his target. He circled to the opposite side of the room, positioning himself behind a marble column where the shadows gathered. The Deceiver's presence at Carver's lecture confirmed Thomas's worst fears, they had detected the quantum resonance signature of the watch. Carver's innocent archaeological discovery was to them a beacon, a siren call promising devastating power. Thomas's fingers brushed against the single gold watch nestled in his inner pocket, its metal warm against his skin despite the January chill. Four decades of searching had yielded only this one, the compass rose watch he'd inherited from Simon. The other four remained scattered across continents, hidden beneath layers of history and encryption that even he, with all his Protector training, had failed to penetrate.

Thomas's heart hammered against his ribs as he edged around the corner, pressing his body flat against the wall. There–at the far end of the deserted hallway–stood Beck, his silver hair gleaming under the fluorescent lights. The Deceiver's lips moved in urgent conversation with another man whose face remained hidden. Thomas's mouth went dry. Two Deceivers. Here. Now. The quantum signature must be stronger than he'd calculated. Sweat beaded along his hairline as he calculated his odds against them both–suicide at best, catastrophic at worst. If they captured him, Earth's last defense would crumble. Thomas lunged backward, fingers fumbling with the auditorium door handle. He slipped back inside, dropping into a rear seat, blood roaring in his ears. Through the sea of heads, he spotted Jack Douglas–oblivious, vulnerable, crucial to everything. Thomas's hand instinctively touched the watch in his pocket. He'd have one chance when Carver finished. One opportunity before the Deceivers closed in. The fate of humanity might depend on the next fifteen minutes.

Carver's lecture wound down as Beck's companion slipped into the auditorium, taking a seat near the front on Thomas's side. Thomas studied the man's profile–definitely younger than Beck, with features he'd never encountered in his decades of surveillance. A new generation of Deceivers. The realization settled like lead in Thomas's stomach. For every one he eliminated, another emerged from whatever dark corner of the universe spawned them. His shoulders sagged momentarily before he straightened his spine. No. The sacrifices of his fallen comrades demanded perseverance, regardless of the odds.

When the audience began filing out, Thomas melded into the stream of bodies, drifting toward where Beck waited in the hallway. He felt no concern about being recognized–Beck had never seen his face, not directly. Thomas's greatest weapon had always been his remarkable ordinariness, a chameleon-like quality honed through centuries of training. While Simon had been the visible hero who thwarted Beck's schemes during the war, Thomas had operated in the shadows. He could engage someone in conversation and minutes later, they'd struggle to recall even the color of his eyes. This invisibility had served the Protectors well, but now Thomas faced an impossible calculation: he needed Jack Douglas, needed to drag the young man into this ancient war. But first, he had to track Beck and his companion. Jack would have to wait.

As Jack leaned forward in his seat, Professor Carver projected the high-resolution image of the gold pocket watch onto the auditorium screen, its intricate engravings catching the light. The ancient symbols etched along the rim–neither Egyptian nor Sumerian, yet somehow familiar–sent a shiver of recognition down Jack's spine. He'd spent countless nights in his bedroom poring over dog-eared copies of von Däniken and Hancock, tracing his finger over photographs of Nazca lines and the impossibly precise stonework of Puma Punku. Not that he believed in stereotypical bug-eyed aliens, but the evidence was compelling: the Ezekiel wheel descriptions in the Bible, the vimanas of ancient Hindu texts, those curious elongated skulls from Peru. Jack's pulse quickened as Carver pointed to the watch's unusual atomic structure, visible in the electron microscope images–proof, perhaps, that someone had been guiding humanity's development since before recorded history.

Jack stuffed his notebook into his backpack and zipped it closed. Time to meet Kevin at the wings place, where he'd inevitably spend the next hour listening to his friend's theories about Julie's supposed attraction to him–despite Kevin's girlfriend at BU and Julie's well-known relationship with the hockey team's center forward. As Jack navigated through the dispersing crowd, he paused near Mr. Carver's impromptu post-lecture gathering. A tall man with unnaturally perfect posture leaned toward the professor, his voice carrying just enough for Jack to catch fragments about examining the gold watch in person. Jack's pulse quickened–he'd give anything for a closer look at that artifact, to verify his suspicions about its otherworldly origins. But Carver's response, floating across the room as Jack pushed through the exit door, dashed those hopes: the watch remained securely locked away in the professor's research facility.

Jack dismissed the overheard conversation as he stepped into Boston's frigid evening air, where fat snowflakes drifted beneath streetlamps. Tomorrow's exam dominated his thoughts–a test he felt confident about but would review anyway, after satisfying his growling stomach. He tugged his jacket tighter and flipped up his collar against the biting wind, then quickened his pace toward the wings place where Kevin waited.

Kevin smirked as Jack slid into the booth across from him. "So, did Carver bring any little green men as visual aids?"

Jack flicked a wadded napkin at Kevin's forehead. "You know, you might actually learn something if you sat through an entire lecture for once."

"Why bother?" Kevin's eyes tracked Julie as she moved between tables, pitcher of water in hand. "Look who's working our section tonight. Told you this was worth missing alien history."

Jack shook his head. "Weren't you taking Ann out Friday? The girl you're supposedly dating?"

"Relax. She's at some family wedding until next week." Kevin's attention remained fixed on Julie as she leaned over a nearby table. "Besides, last I checked, I don't have a ring on my finger."

"And that's exactly why no girl sticks around longer than a month," Jack said, unable to suppress a laugh despite himself. Kevin's eyes followed Julie as she refilled water glasses three tables over. "Life's too short to limit yourself to just one flavor," he said with a smirk.

Jack didn't look up from the laminated menu. "Is that what they're calling it these days?" He flipped the page, weighing buffalo against honey barbecue. "Pretty sure that philosophy's why Ann almost broke up with you last month."

Thomas melted into the shadows across from the Marriott's gleaming glass entrance, his breath forming small clouds in the January air as he tracked the Deceivers. Beck's silver-haired figure moved with unnatural precision through the revolving door, his younger companion following with the fluid grace that marked their kind. Thomas's fingers, numb with cold, gripped the worn brick corner of the building as he debated his next move. The hotel's golden light spilled onto the snow-dusted sidewalk, creating a deceptive warmth that didn't reach his bones. After twenty minutes of surveillance, Thomas abandoned his post, his decision crystallizing like ice. Carver was the key–find the professor, secure the watch.

The lecture hall stood nearly deserted now, its double doors reflecting Thomas's haggard face as he approached. Inside, fluorescent lights buzzed overhead, illuminating empty rows of blue seats. A janitor's mop slapped rhythmically against the linoleum near the podium where Carver had stood hours before. Thomas's shoulders slumped. He retreated to the bitter night and extracted a sleek obsidian device from his pocket–paper-thin, with a surface that rippled like liquid under his touch. The screen cast an eerie blue glow across his weathered features as information about Carver scrolled past his eyes: University of Chicago, tomorrow, 8 PM. The watch, however, lay sealed in darkness three hundred miles away, nestled in the reinforced vault beneath Washington's Museum of Science and Industry.

As Thomas's taxi navigated Boston's slick streets toward Logan, Beck and his companion were already settling into first-class seats on Flight 1782 to Washington, their eyes gleaming with the cold calculation of predators who had just located their prey.

Chapter 12

Ulm, Germany
December 1942

Simon had not realized just how hungry he had been until he sat down in the small restaurant inside the inn. The food was common German fare with breaded veal, boiled potatoes and cucumber salad; it was a welcome change from the train food that Simon had been relegated to. There was little conversation during the meal, and this allowed Simon's thoughts to drift back to his family in Maine and what they must be going through at this moment. He knew that what he was doing was real and that Mr. Grant was indeed telling him the truth, but he still didn't know his full role in all of this. Still the thought of leaving his family was still very much on his mind.

With the meal finished, Mr. Grant broke Simon from his thoughts of home and his young son George, "come Mr. Douglas let us return upstairs, there is much to be covered, and our time is running short with each passing moment.

Back in Simon's room, the two men settled into chairs by the window. The afternoon sun cast long shadows across the worn floorboards as Mr. Grant leaned forward, his voice dropping to just above a whisper. "The Deceivers aren't newcomers to your world," he said, eyes fixed on Simon. "Twenty-five arrived millennia ago. Only seven remain alive today, though their numbers have grown through reproduction." He paused, fingers drumming against his knee. "When they mate with each other, their offspring inherit their longevity. It's only when they breed with humans that their children live normal human lifespans, nearly indistinguishable from the rest of humanity."

Throughout human history, a shadow war has raged. The Protectors fought to shield an innocent species while the Deceivers orchestrated its subjugation. Thomas's predecessors had hunted the Deceivers relentlessly, claiming victories but suffering devastating losses. The past century had seen an escalation–the Deceivers' fingerprints on the American Civil War, World War I, the Russian Revolution, and countless other historical inflection points. Each time humanity teetered on the brink, the Protectors had intervened. Now only Thomas Grant remained, a solitary guardian against their machinations. The Deceivers remained unaware of a crucial truth: with Thomas's eventual death, no more Protectors would follow. The fate of humanity would hang in the balance, with no one left to counter their influence.

Mr. Grant extended his hand. “May I examine your watch again?”

Simon relinquished the timepiece. Mr. Grant turned it over repeatedly, studying its contours before simultaneously twisting the winding knob and opening the face. Instead of the expected gears and springs, Simon saw a small black square no larger than a thumbnail and a tiny circular aperture resembling an eye.

When Mr. Grant adjusted the watch’s hands, the device emitted a soft glow. Suddenly, a three-dimensional image materialized in the air between them–so vivid and substantial that Simon nearly reached out to touch it. The projection displayed text in symbols reminiscent of Egyptian hieroglyphics. As Mr. Grant continued manipulating the knob, the projected images shifted and transformed.

“This single watch houses one-fifth of our world’s collective knowledge–our writings, technology, and historical records,” Mr. Grant explained. Simon frowned. “But I was under the impression it functioned as both a communication tool and transportation device?”

Mr. Grant’s fingers traced the edge of the watch. “Indeed, those were among its capabilities. But when our sun collapsed, everything changed. The portal connecting our worlds sealed permanently. These five devices–they were engineered specifically for transit between your planet and mine.” His voice grew hollow. “Even the communication function is useless now. It was designed solely to bridge messages between our world and whoever wielded the watch here.” He fell silent, his eyes fixed on some distant point beyond the room walls, as if searching for a home that no longer existed. There was a moment of silence between them, this allowed Simon to realize that Mr. Grant had also sacrificed much to try to stop the Deceivers and that knowing that he would never be able to set foot on his home planet again must be a very sobering feeling. Simon could not imagine, nor did he even want the thought of never seeing his family again to enter his mind, it was more than he could bear to imagine.

Mr. Grant’s voice grew tighter as he continued explaining the watch’s purpose. “We discovered a critical vulnerability almost immediately,” he said, running his thumb along the golden edge of the timepiece. “When the first five Protectors arrived on Earth, the Deceivers hunted them like animals through ancient forests and across barren deserts. The watches–these repositories of our civilization–became their primary target.” His eyes darkened as he gazed at the floating image, its blue-green light casting eerie shadows across his weathered face.

"Four Protectors managed to conceal their watches moments before their deaths, burying them beneath stone monuments or sealing them in forgotten caves. But one watch—" he paused, his knuckles whitening around the device, "–one fell into Deceiver hands, giving them fragments of knowledge to recreate our world's technology." From his pocket, Mr. Grant withdrew a small obsidian case that seemed to absorb the surrounding light. "Later Protectors carried these protective shells," he explained, demonstrating how the watch nestled perfectly inside. "They're genetically encoded to the original user–in any other hands, they remain dormant." Simon barely heard the words, transfixed by the shimmering hologram suspended in the air between them, its alien symbols rotating slowly like celestial bodies.

Mr. Grant leaned forward, his voice dropping to a confidential tone. "Unlike us, the Deceivers were politicians, not scientists. They could operate our technology but lacked the expertise to replicate it. Still, the few devices they smuggled to Earth were enough to establish dominion over ancient civilizations."

Simon frowned, running a hand through his hair. "But if your kind has walked among us for two millennia, why hasn't anyone uncovered the truth? How have the Deceivers hidden their agenda all this time?"

A knowing smile played across Mr. Grant's weathered face. "Professor Douglas, the evidence has always been in plain sight." He tapped his finger against the table. "Your ancient texts document our conflict with remarkable clarity. The clues are scattered throughout human history–you simply lacked the context to recognize them."

Simon stared at Mr. Grant with a puzzled look, "What do you mean our ancient..." before Simon even finished his thought it hit him like a ton of bricks, it was all right in there, the Old Testament was filled with references to flying chariots and all of the other religions were filled with god like people descending from the sky to interact with humans, even some of the drawings found in caves all over the world had drawings of aliens and flying objects. A chill ran down Simon's spine as it all seemed to make sense he had always believed but didn't realize just how obvious the signs had been. Mr. Grant's lips curved into a slight smile. "You've made the connections rather quickly, Professor Douglas.

He leaned forward, twisting the watch's knob with practiced precision. The holographic display shifted, revealing intricate schematics of what appeared to be aircraft designs unlike anything Simon had ever seen.

“This particular device contains the fundamentals of flight technology and advanced aerodynamics,” Mr. Grant explained, his voice dropping to a near whisper. “The watch the Deceivers acquired focuses on energy manipulation and biological sciences. In the wrong hands, even fragments of this knowledge can alter the course of human history–as you've already witnessed.” “But why would you put all of this information into these watches and send it with the protectors, why not just send them with weapons?” Simon asked a bit perplexed. If he could see the flawed thinking of Mr. Grant's people surely there had been someone from his home world that could have seen the danger in sending this information here with the chance it could fall into the wrong hands.

“What is knowledge, but power and with knowledge all things can be accomplished,” Mr. Grant calmly answered Simon.

“This is a very powerful weapon; more powerful than any other weapon we could possibly come armed with. The Protectors were sent to your world armed with vast amounts of knowledge and it is all right here at our fingertips, we could never hope to hunt down and kill all the Deceivers. You remember they came to this world and were here for many hundreds of years before we realized what was starting to happen and sent the Protectors to counter what was taking place here. The Deceivers had for many years been growing in number and as you remember our life span is quite long in comparison to that of humans, and when we bred with humans the life span of our offspring is that of a human. When one from my planet breeds with another from our planet then our long-life span will continue. When the first protectors arrived here there had been many years of expansion by the Deceivers and by the time we arrived there were hundreds if not thousands here,” Mr. Grant was interrupted by the sound of an Air Raid siren sounding.

Mr. Grant quickly shut the face of the watch and slid the black case into his inner pocket, “Here take your watch and come quickly,” Mr. Grant said as he stood and moved to the door of the room.

Simon and Mr. Grant quickly made their way to the basement of the Inn with the other guests to wait for all clear.

“It is not likely that the Allied bombing mission is set for Ulm,” Mr. Grant said to Simon as they stood in the basement near the coal furnace. Mr. Grant leaned close to Simon's ear. “The Allies wouldn't waste resources on Ulm,” he whispered. “No strategic targets worth the fuel and bombs.”

An hour later, the all-clear siren wailed. Weary guests shuffled toward the stairs. Simon's eyelids felt like sandpaper as he trudged back to his room. Mr. Grant's assessment had proven correct–no explosions had rocked the city. Simon wondered briefly why Ulm had been spared the devastation visited upon other German towns, but exhaustion quickly overwhelmed his curiosity.

Chapter 13

Cambridge, Massachusetts
January 2001

With hours to spare before his Chicago flight, Thomas claimed a seat near the gate at Boston's Logan Airport. He held the Globe open before him, but his eyes barely registered the headlines. His mind raced through scenarios to recover the watch, then returning to continue his conversation with Jack. Last night's coincidence still unsettled him. After decades of searching, how had he stumbled upon both a missing watch's location and two Deceivers on the same evening? Thomas hunched behind his newspaper at the airport gate, peering out over the crumpled edge with a predator's patience. The terminal was a cathedral to human restlessness–steel beams and security glass, all the rituals of modern travel performed by restless, shuffling acolytes. He scanned every face, searching for the angular features and pale hair of Beck, or the companion who'd moved with such calculated silence the night before. Instead, threading through the crowd with a careful, almost apologetic gait, was Mr. Carver, the academic who'd unwittingly become the fulcrum of Thomas's entire mission.

Carver stood at the check-in kiosk, squinting at the digital prompts, and then drifted to the gate with a rolling briefcase. He wore a brown corduroy sport coat and moved with the conspicuous nervousness of someone new to air travel, checking his pocket watch and then the scrolling gate display. The gesture struck Thomas as both perfectly ordinary and given last night's revelations, a grim sort of poetry.

But where were Beck and the brute?

Thomas had expected them to shadow Carver with the relentless subtlety of professionals. Instead, there was no trace–no hint of the two Deceivers. He stared at the gate area: a mother soothing a howling toddler, two college boys debating whether to pre-board, a bored gate agent chewing her pen at the counter. No sign.

Thomas's instincts, honed over centuries, screamed at him: This was not luck.

He rose and circled the waiting area as if searching for an outlet to charge his phone, winding his way past Carver, who seemed too absorbed in his own private anxieties to notice. Thomas scanned every face, every slumped body in a Logan Airport chair, every shadow flitting behind a food kiosk. Beck and his companion were not here. Thomas forced himself to think like them–to consider their options, their tactics. If they'd lost interest in Carver, it was only because they'd found something better. Or worse, someone had already extracted the necessary information.

A boarding announcement jolted the gate area into sudden movement. The crowd surged toward the jetway, and in the crush of bodies Thomas felt the old, familiar sense of vulnerability. So much could be staged in these tight quarters: a subtle handoff, a bag slipped into the wrong overhead bin, a needle prick at the elbow. He checked his own carry-on just to be sure–everything was untouched, the small black case still perfectly nested below his folded shirt.

Carver entered the line just ahead of Thomas, glancing over his shoulder as if expecting an old friend or an old debt. Thomas kept his gaze low, studying the interplay of anxiety and anticipation on Carver's face. The man was jumpy, but not paranoid. He did not look like someone being followed. Which meant the wolves had scented a juicier trail elsewhere.

Thomas considered doubling back to the main concourse, searching the other gates, but he hesitated. If the Deceivers had shifted priorities, the only logical destination was the next known location of the watch–or, failing that, the people most likely to reconstruct its secrets. For now, that meant Thomas's best play was to stick to Carver and wait for a break. He scanned the boarding line one final time, looking for the flicker of a familiar face, the shimmer of a gun under a coat, a bulge in a messenger bag. Nothing. The absence was too perfect, too surgical. It reeked of strategic withdrawal.

As the line shuffled forward, Thomas felt a strange kinship with Carver, both men moving toward a fate that neither fully understood, both haunted by secrets encoded in the ticking of ancient devices. He recalled the weight of his own watch, heavy with the accumulated failures of his predecessors, and wondered if Carver had the faintest inkling of what he had found in those jungles in Central America.

The jetway air was a different kind of stale–compressed, metallic, filled with the nervous chatter of strangers forced into proximity. Thomas boarded, stowed his bag, and took his seat near the front. From there, he could see the length of the cabin. Carver was five rows behind, already fussing with the window shade, his knuckles white on the armrest.

Thomas buckled in, the ritual both calming and absurd. After five centuries navigating the worst humanity had to offer–wars, plagues, betrayals–it was still commercial aviation that made his palms sweat. He often fantasized about priming some piece of discarded Prellian technology to make these primitive flights obsolete, to spare himself the indignity of trusting his life to the lowest bidder's maintenance schedule. But for now, he was stuck with the same cattle-car anxiety as every other traveler.

He let the drone of safety announcements wash over him, eyes closed, senses tuned to the smallest ripple in the cabin. If Beck or his companion had made the flight, they would be near the exits, positioned for maximum control but minimum attention. But as the flight attendants counted heads and closed the main door, Thomas knew they weren't on board. Not even in disguise. They'd shifted the game board, and Thomas was flying blind.

He tried to settle his mind–review the clues, reconstruct the timeline–but found himself instead reliving the memory of Mr. Grant in that 1942 inn, the haunted look on the old man's face as he explained the stakes to a much younger Simon. How many times have the Protectors underestimated their foes? How many times had the Deceivers slipped past, unseen, leaving only catastrophe in their wake?

Thomas closed his eyes and felt the engines rumble to life, the plane shuddering down the tarmac. He wondered, for the thousandth time, whether this was the flight that would end him–not in a crash, well that was still a real possibility but, no he was thinking about the potential of catastrophic oversight, one last failure to anticipate the enemy's real move.

The cabin lights dimmed for takeoff. Thomas forced himself to breathe, to focus. He would use these next two hours to replay every interaction, every word, every gesture from the museum. Perhaps he'd missed something. Perhaps he could still get ahead of Beck, if only by the smallest margin.

And so, the plane lifted into the winter sky, trailing its thin line of hope and dread across the continent.

Thomas settled into his seat near the front; he saw that Mr. Carver was about five seats behind him. Now all he had to do was block out the idea that he was flying in this tin can of death.

Just as the plane pushed back from the gate, the realization hit Thomas like ice water. Beck and his companion weren't on this flight because they no longer needed Carver. The truth burned in his mind:

they'd discovered the watch's location through other means. Thomas gripped the armrest, his knuckles whitening beneath five centuries of weathered skin. How could he have been so careless? He should have never let those two predators slip from his sight. Now his only fragile hope was to shadow Carver across the continent, praying the nervous professor would unknowingly lead him to the ancient device before the Deceivers could claim it. The plane's engines whined higher as they taxied, each second carrying him farther from whatever critical clue he'd overlooked during the lecture.

"May I offer you something to drink, sir?" A young flight attendant with copper hair and tired eyes leaned into his peripheral vision, her practiced smile barely masking the exhaustion of her third consecutive flight. Thomas swallowed the bitter truth he wanted to speak: Not unless you can turn this metal coffin around and take me back to the terminal where I belong.

"Just water, thank you," he replied instead, his voice carrying the polite restraint of centuries.

Thomas couldn't shake the prickling at the back of his neck–the certainty that he'd overlooked something crucial, and that Beck and his companion were already a step ahead. He sat rigidly in the pressurized cabin, fluorescent ceiling panels humming overhead, and reached into his jacket pocket for the small black case. Its matte surface was cool against his palm, a reminder that in this race nothing remained hidden for long.

Around him, the plane's engines droned–a direct legacy of the Deceivers, who had quietly armed the Nazi war machine with the first workable jet engine. Thomas remembered how he and Simon had sabotaged the project in 1944, halting its evolution and leaving humanity with a half-finished design. Now, ironically, that same leap in technology let him use the thin black device most any place and he took it from his pocket. He often wondered if the Protectors, in their desperate bid to contain the Deceivers, hadn't only fueled humanity's hunger for progress. Every new gizmo he unlocked to counter Beck's schemes only nudged civilization farther from its natural course.

He angled his head, taking in the cabin's stale air, the dull thrum of turbines vibrating through the armrest, the fellow passengers dozing under blankets. On the bulkhead screen ahead, the flight path arced toward Chicago. A pale blue glow washed across his face as his finger swiped through archived dossiers, coded manifests, half-forgotten memos. He hunted for the clue that had escaped him, though he couldn't say exactly what form it would take.

Row after row of files offered nothing definitive. His chest tightened with each fruitless swipe while the skyline of Lake Michigan drew nearer. Then–buried in a footnote from a routine security clearance–he found it: a passing mention of Mr. Carver's appointment to a high-level research post in Washington, D.C. No fanfare, just a line tucked between budget forecasts. But Thomas's heart seized. This had to be it. Carver was guarding the watch in his new lab, and Beck would be there soon.

After landing Thomas shouldered his way through the terminal crowd, self-recrimination burning in his chest. Five centuries of vigilance, and still he'd missed what was right before him. He scanned the departure board–a flight to Washington D.C. leaving in thirty minutes. A slim chance, perhaps his only one. The question that twisted his gut wasn't whether he could make the flight, but whether Beck was already holding the watch in his hands.

When the boarding call came, Thomas found himself crammed into a seat by the lavatories. The engines whined as they taxied, and through the small oval window, he watched the same stretch of concrete he'd traversed less than an hour ago slip beneath the wing. Five hundred years of life, and here he was, chasing his own tail.

The wind howled across campus as Jack hurried back from dinner with Kevin. Though the snow had stopped, bitter gusts sliced through his jacket while he passed the library. Mr. Carver's lecture about the gold watch consumed his thoughts. Could an alien artifact really exist? And what might that mean for everything humanity believed about its history? Jack needed answers. He quickened his pace and yanked his collar higher, desperate for any barrier against the biting cold.

Once inside the warmth of his dorm, Jack immediately reached for his phone.

"Mom? Is Dad around?" he asked when she answered.

"Jack! How are you doing, sweetheart?"

"Fine, just freezing," he replied, rubbing his free hand against his arm to restore circulation. "That wind out there is brutal."

"Is Dad around? I need to ask him about something."

"Oh, you know where he is–glued to that computer since Kevin set up the internet," his mother sighed. "That man hasn't seen daylight in hours."

"Could you get him for me?"

"Hold on, I'll drag him away from his precious screen," she said with a hint of affection beneath her exasperation.

"Thanks, Mom. Love you."

Dad's voice crackled through the receiver. "Jack! What's going on, son?"

Jack smiled, picturing his father hunched at his desk, the blue glow of the monitor illuminating his face. Ever since Kevin had set up their home internet connection three months ago, George Douglas had transformed into a digital archaeologist, excavating historical facts until well past midnight.

"Nothing much. Just got back from Carver's lecture," Jack said, dropping his backpack on the floor. "The one I mentioned yesterday?"

"Carver, right." The familiar click-click of a mouse carried through the phone. "Been reading up on him all afternoon. Found some fascinating stuff about his research." Jack clutched the phone tighter. "Dad, that's actually why I'm calling. In your research, have you ever come across anything about a gold watch connected to... well, aliens?"

"I have, actually," his father replied without hesitation. "After you mentioned Carver's lecture, I got curious. Did some digging online." The familiar sound of keyboard clicking came through the receiver. "Turns out he just accepted a government position–special research director of some kind. There were articles mentioning a gold watch he discovered in Mayan ruins in Mexico. Claims it's extraterrestrial... and still functioning."

"But before today–had you ever heard of anything like this?" Jack pressed, pacing across his dorm room.

His father's voice lowered slightly. "Only vague references. Something about five watches that have supposedly been on Earth since ancient times. The scholarly literature barely mentions them."

"But do you think–" Jack couldn't help interrupting, "–could Carver's claims actually be legitimate?"

George's voice dropped to a near whisper. "That's just it, Jack. There's barely a footnote about these watches in legitimate journals.

But I found something else–an obscure forum post from a man in Ulm, Germany. His writing was... unsettling. Meticulous details about alien factions battling over these gold watches across millennia. The screen glowed with his words as I read until three this morning." George paused, the sound of papers shuffling came through the receiver. "He describes his grandfather's gnarled hands trembling as he recounted meeting what he called 'the Protectors'–benevolent aliens with eyes that reflected starlight. According to the account, a tall alien named Thomas and a human companion arrived at his grandfather's snow-covered inn during the darkest days of the war.

"This man claims that each watch could unlock untold advances in technology," George continued, his voice tense with excitement. "Blueprints etched into atomic structures, visible only through devices the aliens themselves designed."

"Do you believe any of it?" Jack asked, gripping the phone so tightly his knuckles whitened.

George cleared his throat. "Carver has a solid reputation–doesn't make unfounded claims. But this German fellow from Ulm? The academic community dismisses him as delusional. He promises evidence but delivers nothing except fantastical narratives."

"Still," George continued, his voice dropping thoughtfully, "the coincidence is striking. Both men fixated on these gold watches."

"You think Carver might be onto something real?" Jack leaned against his desk.

"If he is, then we can't simply ignore Walker's accounts either." George tapped his fingers rhythmically on his desk. "Two unconnected sources, same obscure artifact–that's not random chance."

"Going to keep digging, aren't you?" Jack smiled into the phone, picturing his father's furrowed brow, the look that always appeared when he'd caught the scent of a historical mystery.

"You know me too well," George chuckled. "I'll follow this thread wherever it leads."

"Let me know what you find out and I'll talk to you after our game on Friday," Jack said, already knowing who he needed to ask for help on finding out more about these watches.

"Will do, son. Good luck with the Northeastern game–show those

Huskies what Harvard is made of," George replied, his voice warm with pride before the line clicked dead.

Jack stood motionless in his cramped dorm room, staring at the peeling corner of his Neil Armstrong poster. The fluorescent ceiling light cast harsh shadows across his unmade bed while the radiator clanked and hissed beneath the frost-rimmed window. Five gold watches scattered across continents, each one potentially holding secrets beyond human comprehension. The thought sent electric shivers down his spine. Were there really aliens walking among them, locked in an ancient conflict that had shaped human history? His pulse quickened as he imagined the watches' intricate gears turning, perhaps powered by energy unknown to science.

Jack's gaze drifted to Kevin's dorm just down the hall, its window glowing amber against the night. Kevin had the computer skills to dig deeper but convincing him would require more than wild theories about extraterrestrial timepieces.

Chapter 14

Ulm, Germany
December 1942

The air raid warning had just been lifted when Simon heard a soft knock at his door. He knew it would be Mr. Grant, eager to resume their interrupted conversation. Opening the door, Simon found the man standing in the dim hallway, expression tense. Simon ushered him inside and closed the door behind them. As they moved toward the sitting area, Simon reached for the small lamp between the chairs, but Mr. Grant's hand shot out to stop him.

"Keep it dark," Mr. Grant whispered, moving to the window to verify the shade was completely lowered. "We can't risk drawing attention." "Sit down; let me fill you in," Mr. Grant said, gesturing to the chair. Simon settled into it. "You asked why we risked sending the five watches here, knowing they might fall into the wrong hands. Frankly, it was a mistake. We assumed the Deceivers would never find them–but, as you know, they did, but with some luck we were able to hide the watches just before the Deceivers captured them. What they didn't realize is that those five watches were only part of the puzzle. There's a sixth component, the golden box, sent just before our sun reached its final stage. If the Deceivers ever find it, they could unlock powers and technologies beyond anything imaginable–capable of both devastating destruction and miraculous creation, depending entirely on the user's intent."

Mr. Grant paused, rose, and crossed to the door. He peered down the hallway before returning and closing it softly. Leaning in, he lowered his voice to a whisper. "The box's power is so immense that simply holding it isn't enough to access its full potential. Only by bringing together all five watches with the box can one command its complete force. Even so, the box alone is far more potent than any single watch."

Clearing his throat, Mr. Grant went on, "Shortly after its arrival, the Deceivers discovered it. They nearly seized it, but it slipped away–and no one's seen it since. We do know they're still searching, which means they don't have it... yet."

Simon shook his head. "With all due respect, Mr. Grant, your people have a remarkable talent for losing critical items."

A genuine smile spread across Mr. Grant's face as he chuckled. "Mr.

Douglas, you're absolutely right."

Simon leaned forward. "You showed me a photo of my grandfather and said he helped defeat the Deceivers during the First World War. What happened to him? And why have you come to me for help?"

Mr. Grant's expression turned serious. "I did. It's vital you understand everything before we leave this room tomorrow. Your life–and mine–and the fate of the world depend on it."

Chapter 15

Cambridge, Massachusetts
January 2001

Jack snatched up his phone, fingers trembling slightly as he punched in Kevin's number. The digital clock on his nightstand glowed 11:45 PM, but Jack knew his longtime friend wouldn't be asleep, he'd be hunched over his custom-built computer rig with its three monitors and pulsing blue LED lights, fingers dancing across the keyboard as he tinkered with one of his many custom-made programs that were quite possibly illegal. The phone rang four times, each ring stretching Jack's nerves tighter.

"Hello?" Kevin's voice came through breathless, with rustling sheets audible in the background.

"Hey man, I need your help on something urgent," Jack said, pacing across his cramped dorm room. "I need you to work that computer magic of yours–the kind that makes the FBI nervous."

"First thing tomorrow morning," Kevin whispered, his words clipped and hurried.

"What's wrong with now?" Jack stopped by his window, staring at the snow-dusted campus below. "You're clearly awake, and I want to hit this while the trail's still hot."

"Morning would just be better," Kevin hissed. "I'm a little... occupied at the moment, if you catch my drift." A feminine giggle filtered through the phone.

"I thought Ann was visiting her parents this weekend?" Jack's eyebrows shot up.

"Yes, that's right," Kevin replied, his tone deliberately neutral.

"Oh man, you're unbelievable," Jack shook his head, running a hand through his disheveled hair. "Who've you got over there now? Actually–wait–I don't want to know."

"Just throw some clothes on and get over here," Jack insisted, his voice dropping to a serious tone. "This is important, Kevin. Life-changing important."

"Fine, fine," Kevin sighed dramatically. "Ten minutes. This better be worth it." The line went dead as Kevin turned to the slender figure beside him. "Julie, I've gotta go."

Chapter 16

Washington, D.C.
January 2001

The plane touched down at Washington National Airport with a jolt that made Thomas grip his armrests. As the roar of the engines faded, he released a long-held breath. These primitive flying machines–how many more decades would humans waste perfecting them? The answer to true flight wasn't in these petroleum-guzzling monstrosities, but in principles so obvious they might as well be written in the sky. If only they could see beyond their oil-soaked vision, Thomas thought, gathering his briefcase as passengers around him stood to retrieve their belongings.

How much of a head start did Beck have in his quest to take the watch? Thomas wondered, his leather shoes clicking against the polished floor of the jetway as fluorescent lights buzzed overhead. The terminal sprawled before him; a cavernous space dotted with red-eye, weary travelers clutching coffee cups and overnight bags. Time was a razor-thin margin now–a commodity as precious as the artifact he sought. The watch had to be in Carver's office, that windowless vault three floors beneath the Museum of Science and Industry's marble halls, probably tucked behind a false panel or nestled in a wall safe with a combination known only to its keeper. Thomas adjusted his tie, feeling the weight of his own watch against his wrist, a pale imitation of the power contained in the one he pursued.

As Thomas's polished oxfords hit the terminal floor, Beck and his companion, Mike Gray, stood motionless in the shadow of the Museum of Science and Industry's neoclassical columns. The massive building loomed against the star-speckled sky, its windows dark except for the faint security lights that cast long, distorted shadows across the manicured lawn. It was 3 AM, the air heavy with pre-dawn moisture that clung to their skin. Their plan, meticulously crafted during the flight to Washington D.C., pulsed in their minds with crystalline clarity.

Thomas's cab sliced through the empty streets, its headlights briefly illuminating a bronze statue before pulling up to the curb. A gnarled oak tree, its branches twisting like arthritic fingers, obscured the two figures lurking twenty yards away. As Thomas paid the driver, the cab's interior light illuminated his face in a harsh yellow glow. Beck's eyes narrowed, his hand instinctively touching the cold metal weapon concealed beneath his charcoal suit jacket. The cab pulled away with a soft purr, leaving Thomas alone on the sidewalk. Beck watched the solitary figure approach, moonlight catching on Thomas's silver tie clip. Something electric sparked in Beck's memory–that measured gait, the squared shoulders. Though he couldn't place the face, recognition itched at the back of his mind like a half-forgotten nightmare.

Thomas had taken only three steps when he spotted the silhouettes against the museum's granite facade–two men standing motionless in the shadows cast by the towering oak. Their stillness was predatory, deliberate. In the silver wash of moonlight, Thomas recognized Beck's angular jawline and the glint of something metallic in Gray's hand.

Beck's lips moved, his whisper carried away by the night breeze. Gray pivoted with unnatural speed, raising what looked like an antique pistol with strange modifications. A pulse of cobalt energy erupted from the barrel, bathing the walkway in electric blue. Thomas's retinas seared white-hot as the world disappeared into blinding light.

Thomas's vision hadn't yet returned when the second blast hit him–blue energy that emptied his lungs and left him gasping. Gray advanced with inhuman precision, each movement unnaturally smooth as he delivered a blow to Thomas's temple. Blood misted across his attacker's immaculate coat buttons. Thomas managed to graze his hidden weapon with trembling fingers before a third blast lifted him off his feet. His spine cracked against the gnarled oak that had concealed his enemies, the same tree whose shadow had hidden the ambush until it was too late.

Paralysis gripped him, every nerve ending screaming in silent agony. His fingers twitched uselessly as he struggled to reach the device in his breast pocket. Gray approached, his footsteps crunching on fallen leaves, the modified weapon now humming with an otherworldly resonance. The barrel glowed blue-white as Gray took aim at Thomas's forehead, and then consciousness slipped away like water through cupped hands.

"Mike! The cameras will have caught that flash. Police response time in this district is under three minutes," Beck hissed, his voice tight with urgency.

Gray crouched beside Thomas's crumpled form, fingers searching for a pulse beneath the blood-slicked collar. "Strange–he seems familiar. Let me check his identification."

The distant wail of sirens cut through the night air just as Gray's fingers closed around Thomas's wallet. Beck yanked his companion upright by his expensive lapel. "Leave it! The watch is our priority, not this corpse," he snarled, eyes darting toward the approaching lights.

They vanished into the dense shrubbery bordering the museum grounds, their expensive shoes leaving no prints on the dewy grass. As Beck slipped through a gap in the wrought-iron fence, he heard the squeal of brakes and an officer's voice calling for medical assistance. "Still breathing! Get an ambulance here now!"

Beck permitted himself a small smile as the darkness swallowed them whole.

Chapter 17

Cambridge, Massachusetts
January 2001

Kevin barged into Jack's dorm room at 12 AM, his hair disheveled and his shirt half-untucked. "This better be good," he said, flopping onto Jack's unmade bed. "Julie wasn't exactly thrilled when I got your text." Jack rolled his eyes. "Julie Pearson? Waters' girlfriend? Seriously?" Kevin shrugged with a self-satisfied smile. "What can I say? I've got a gift."

Jack leaned forward in his desk chair. "Remember that gold watch Carver was showing off tonight? The one he swears aliens made?"

"You dragged me away from Julie for some conspiracy theory about a pocket watch?" Kevin jumped to his feet. "I'm going to go see if I can catch up to Julie and pick up where we left off."

"You're staying right here," Jack said, blocking the door. "Unless you want Jason Waters to find out exactly where you were tonight."

"You wouldn't do that, I'm your best friend and you said yourself you don't like that big thug because he is a dirty player on the ice," Kevin said as he grabbed a basketball from the floor and began to toss it in the air.

"Well, you're going to need someone to keep him from killing you when he finds out," Jack said as he snatched the ball from midair.

"Hmm, you're right about that, so what is it I can help you with about these gold watches?" Kevin said as he grinned at Jack, remembering all the times Jack saved his hide from angry boyfriends.

"I spoke with dad tonight and asked him about the gold watches and if there was anything to it. He told me about a few mentions of them in the mainstream academia, but he also told me about the man from Ulm Germany, I think his name was Walker or something, but this man claims to know of these five gold watches and some kind of battle between these good aliens and these bad aliens who want to control the world," Jack explained to Kevin about his conversation with his father.

"I knew I shouldn't have hooked your dad into the net, now he has gone off the reservation with this crazy stuff and taken you with him,"

Kevin added shaking his head, but at the same time a bit curious about what he was hearing.

“I need your help in finding out more about these watches, I want to know if there is anything classified on them and I want to know more about this guy Walker from Ulm who claims that his grandfather knew about these aliens.”

“I need you to use your vast computer skills to find out what you can, I think that this watch Carver was showing us is the real deal and I don’t think that he knows what he has found or what the use of them is for,” Jack told Kevin, knowing Kevin wouldn’t pass up the chance to show off his computer skills.

Kevin had a gift with computers that bordered on the supernatural. His professors were years behind him, and he only stayed enrolled for the diploma–and the dating pool.

“Count me in,” Kevin said, rising to stretch. “Beats watching another professor fumble through a lecture on code I wrote in middle school. I’ll dig around and see what turns up.”

“You want to grab a taco, I’m starved, and late-night exercise makes me hungry,” Kevin said with a grin on his face. “Get out of here you nut,” Jack said as he tossed a shirt at Kevin.

“Ok, I will give you an update tomorrow, meet me at the wing place for dinner,” Kevin said as he tossed the shirt back and headed out the door.

Jack knew that if there was something to find that Kevin would find it, he didn’t know why finding out about the gold watches was so important, there were hundreds of these sorts of claims made every year. You could hardly go a week without someone claiming they had been abducted by aliens or have seen a UFO, and for all he knew a good portion of these claims were true. There was something about this watch that drew his interest and that was enough for now.

Chapter 18

Ulm, Germany
December 1942

Simon sat alone in the darkened room, the window shade pulled up despite the blackout conditions. No light burned inside; he needed only the faint glow of stars to contemplate the impossible. Mr. Grant's revelations echoed in his mind, each one more outlandish than the last, yet supported by evidence too detailed to dismiss. Grant had left him to process everything alone, understanding the weight of such knowledge, while he went to prepare for the dangerous days ahead.

"*I am an Alien??*" Simon whispered to the empty room, testing how the words felt on his tongue. "My father was an Alien. I have Alien blood in me." His fingers traced absent patterns on the wooden armrest as he tried to reconcile his identity as a physics professor from Maine with this new reality–descendant of the Prellians, inheritor of an otherworldly legacy that had brought him to this small inn in Ulm.

Thomas had explained to Simon that his father, William Douglas, was the undisputed leader of the Prellians. In the dying days of their sun, the other Prellian chiefs feared their line would vanish, so they resolved to preserve it–and, when the time came, to leave Earth in search of a new world of their own. Their only guarantee of survival lay in smuggling William to Earth, where he would hide from the Deceivers until he could lead his people to a fresh beginning.

For months William argued fiercely against abandoning his people, insisting his place was with them through their final ordeal. Meanwhile, scouts fanned out across the cosmos in a desperate bid to find a habitable world. Simon recalled that, amid this turmoil, Thomas himself had been sent to Earth as part of the last contingent of protectors. When Thomas departed to battle the Deceivers as part of the last Protectors, William and his wife Doris had already been on earth for years.

William Douglas arrived under the cloak of night, accompanied only by his wife and a single Defender whose sole purpose was to ensure their safety. But it soon became clear that a spy remained among those on Prellia–and that spy had betrayed William's destination. The Deceivers, recognizing him as the greatest threat to their plan to dominate humanity and the surviving Prellians, moved to destroy him. With William dead, they would tighten their grip on both species and crush any hope of rebellion.

Thomas went on to tell Simon how, years before the American Civil War, his father, William, and his wife had quietly settled in Charleston, South Carolina. William took a position as a professor at the local college, while his unseen Protector lived nearby, his presence hidden by design. But the Deceivers had learned William's whereabouts, and before long they were closing in–readying an assault on him and his family.

Chapter 19

Charleston, South Carolina
April 11, 1861

Allan Knight had one mission: protect William Douglas and his wife Doris at all costs. As the appointed guardian of his people's leader, Allan maintained constant vigilance from the shadows. When he spotted two suspicious men watching from across the street, his instincts flared. They'd been found. How the Deceivers had tracked them remained a mystery, but that hardly mattered now. William Douglas wasn't merely a man–he was the hope of Allan's entire race, sent to Earth to live until the last of the scouts that had been sent out into the universe returned in the hopes that they had found a new planet to restart their race. Allan's own life was expendable in service to this greater purpose. Without hesitation, he moved to intercept the threat.

The Deceivers' plan backfired spectacularly. They had anticipated Allan's protective instincts and deliberately created a situation to lure him into the open, where they believed he would be exposed and easily eliminated alongside William Douglas and his wife. What they failed to account for was Allan's combat prowess. Before the Deceivers could even register the threat, Allan had already terminated two of their operatives with lethal efficiency.

Twilight descended as thunderheads gathered on the horizon. Allan faced a dilemma–he needed to warn William but couldn't risk leading the Deceivers to his charge. He veered toward the sea wall along the battery, hoping to eliminate his pursuers before returning to the Douglas home. The wind whipped his coat as he lured the two agents away. Meanwhile, William Douglas arrived home, oblivious to the danger, just as the first heavy raindrops pelted the windows.

Allan's footsteps echoed against the battery wall when the trap sprang. Two Deceivers materialized from the shadows, their movements fluid and predatory. The air crackled as Allan pivoted, dispatching the first attacker with a precise strike to the throat, the second with a sweeping leg maneuver that sent the creature sprawling. But he wasn't fast enough to dodge the third Deceiver's weapon–twin bolts of azure energy seared through his flesh. Rain hissed against his burning wounds as Allan fought on, each movement a testament to his resolve. Thinking his wounds would take care of him, the remaining Deceivers scattered into the storm-shrouded night, leaving their fallen comrades behind.

As Allan assessed his injuries, he spotted a glint of gold on the rain-slicked cobblestones. There, half-concealed beneath the splayed fingers of a fallen enemy, lay one of the watches. He snatched it up, its weight solid and ancient in his palm despite the chaos around him. Crimson rivulets snaked down Allan's torso, soaking his shirt and trousers as each heartbeat pushed more life from the wounds in his chest. The metallic taste of blood filled his mouth as he staggered through Charleston's storm-lashed streets, each labored step leaving a dark trail on the rain-washed pavement. Time was bleeding away with his strength.

By midnight, William and his wife were northbound on a hastily arranged carriage, the golden timepiece nestled in William's pocket–its intricate engravings now obscured by the dried blood of the man who had sacrificed everything to deliver it just hours before, as thunder rolled over his final breaths on William's whitewashed porch.

....

Thomas' account of that night took only a few minutes to tell and by the end Simon, now more than ever, wanted to be back home, to hold his wife and young son George in his arms again. The knowledge Thomas had given Simon had his mind racing trying to understand all of it, he knew that Thomas would be knocking on his door again and their mission to stop the Deceivers would begin.

Chapter 20

Ulm, Germany
December 1942

The knock at Simon's door came precisely at the appointed hour. After a night of revelations, he felt the weight of his birthright settle on his shoulders–a burden he no longer resisted but embraced. Mankind's freedom from the Deceivers now rested partly in his hands.

"Ready for departure, Mr. Douglas?" Thomas stood framed in the doorway, his features subtly altered from the night before. "I think you should call me Simon now," he replied, stepping aside with a welcoming gesture. "After everything you've shared, formalities seem rather pointless." His eyes narrowed slightly as he studied his visitor's face–familiar yet somehow transformed.

"How come you look different this morning?" Simon asked Thomas. "I cannot let any deceiver know what I truly look like, if they figure out who I am, as they almost assuredly will during this mission, they will never stop hunting me, so when this all is done, I will alter my appearance once again," Thomas said as he stood in the center of the room. "You don't look that different, I mean I still knew it was you," Simon said as he looked Thomas over. "Yes, but you knew it was me and were expecting me, the subtle changes are not meant to completely alter my appearance, just enough to look different. Your mind will remember this look and years from now if I were to run across you, you would not be able to remember how I used to look," Thomas explained.

The crunch of their footsteps echoed like distant gunfire in the otherwise silent dawn as Thomas and Simon trudged through knee-deep drifts of virgin snow. Ulm's medieval spires rose around them, black silhouettes against a sky as pale and cold as a corpse. The morning air bit at Simon's lungs with each breath, crystallizing into white plumes that dissipated in the windless air. Neither man spoke as they navigated the cobblestoned square, now transformed into a pristine white canvas unmarred by other travelers. Their destination loomed ahead–a severe red-brick edifice with narrow windows like suspicious eyes watching their approach.

Thomas carried forged papers in his breast pocket that had granted him access to what locals believed was merely a code-breaking facility, though the absence of uniformed personnel and the electrified fencing told a different story. The Nazi Special Science Department operated behind those walls, its secrets guarded by men in civilian clothes with cold eyes and concealed weapons. Thomas had infiltrated this fortress over weeks of careful maneuvering, piecing together the horrifying truth of Deceiver involvement before racing across an ocean and a continent to retrieve Simon from the safety of Maine.

As the two neared the main entrance Thomas once again reminded Simon of what he was to do. "Remember you are here to inspect the progress on the machine, you are head of the Nazi Secret Weapons Division, and your name is Sven Hofferstein. The good thing about the Nazi system is that in a secret program things are kept so secret that even the highest-ranking officers don't question orders from above." Thomas said as they made their way up the front steps. "And since you are not German but rather Swiss your lack of a good German accent will not be any issue since there are many Swiss involved in the war effort here in Germany," Thomas added.

Simon and Thomas entered the door, kicked the snow from their shoes and stepped through a second inner door that opened to a large office area where about a dozen people were working at different desks. They all appeared busy and no one appeared interested in the two men that had just entered the room. Thomas proceeded to the rear of the room to a door labeled supply; the two men entered through the door and into a smaller office where four SS guards were posted.

All were holding weapons and gave off the impression that if you weren't supposed to be here you wouldn't be leaving alive. Simon tried to act as if this were normal and as if he had been through this before; all the while inside he was as scared as he had ever been in his life, one small misstep here and it would be over.

Thomas walked up to the SS guard seated at the small desk in the rear of the office, the Guard appeared to recognize Thomas and they spoke a few words. The guard was short and a bit more round with a reddish tint to his face as if he had been out in the cold or had just overexerted himself. He seemed to like Thomas and asked him how his travels had been and how long he would be staying here on this trip. The guard suggested that they should meet later at the inn for a pint and dinner, and Thomas could tell him about his travels. Then the red-faced man shifted his gaze to Simon and asked for Simon to step forward and present his papers, Thomas stepped to the side to allow Simon to come forward.

This was the moment, if Simon faltered for even a moment, both he and Thomas would not make it out of this room alive. He stepped up to the desk and pulled his papers from his inner pocket and handed them to the guard who took them and glanced at them and then asked Simon what his business was about. Simon quickly responded he was here to check the progress of the machine and assess the level of security for the Fuhrer himself.

The guard quickly stood and handed the papers back to Simon with his apologies and offered to show him around. Simon waved his hand as if to dismiss this request and said he wanted a full report from the lead scientist in charge.

The Guard then immediately picked up the black phone on his desk and asked for Herr Beck to meet him in the main building that Mr. Hofferstein was here at the request of the Fuhrer himself.

The red-faced guard quickly opened the rear door that was flanked by two other SS guards and lead them down a staircase and through another door that opened into a room with four more SS guards with dogs, at the far end of the room were two more doors. Suddenly the two doors burst open and in walked and angry looking man. The red-faced guard snapped to attention. "Herr Beck, may I present Mr. Hofferstein. He requires a full progress report on the machine for the Führer."

A man strode toward them through the doorway–slender, younger than Simon had expected, with hair like polished coal and eyes so dark they seemed to absorb light rather than reflect it. His gaze locked onto Simon with laser precision, sweeping past the guard as though the man were merely furniture. The contempt in his dismissal told Simon everything: this was no subordinate, but the facility's commander himself.

Beck halted inches from Simon's face. "I report directly to the Führer," he said, each word precise as a scalpel. "Who authorized this visit?"

Simon felt a flicker of doubt ignite in his chest.

Chapter 21

Cambridge, Massachusetts/ Washington, D.C.
January 2001

The attending physician at George Washington Hospital shook his head as he reviewed the chart. Thomas Grant shouldn't be alive. The paramedics had found him ten feet from where his shoes still stood, as if some massive electrical force had literally blown him out of his footwear.

Six days later, Thomas remained unconscious. Hospital records identified him as a 42-year-old software engineer from Houston, Texas. The police inventory of his possessions was brief: a featureless black case and a gold pocket watch with a silver key dangling from its chain. With no next of kin located, authorities could only wait for him to regain consciousness and explain what had happened.

Security footage revealed little–just Thomas exiting a cab alone, followed seconds later by a brilliant blue flash that hurled him to the ground. Though it resembled a lightning strike, meteorological records confirmed no electrical storms within three hundred miles of Washington D.C. that night.

The next night following the strange event in front of the Museum of Science and Industry an even stranger event occurred inside the Museum, a robbery took place down three floors below the main Museum floor, and a lone gold watch was taken from the newly occupied offices of Harrison Carver.

Nothing else had been taken; it appeared as if nothing else had even been touched, it was as if the thieves knew what they were after and where to find it.

What was even stranger was the security system, a state-of-the-art system just upgraded seven months prior, looked as if it had been hit with a surge of power so great that it had completely destroyed the system and all its backups in an instant. The head of security systems for all the museums could not explain what had happened; it looked to him as if a direct bolt of lightning had hit the control panel on the southeast corner entrance. When the surveillance video was reviewed the only thing that was visible was a flash of blue light and then all systems went dark.

The headlines of major papers around the country the next morning read "Strange blue light causing concern in the nation's capital". Beck was sitting in his hotel room reading the morning paper just blocks from the museum where only hours before he and Gray had taken the gold watch. He went on reading the story wanting to find out the fate of the man from the night before but there was no mention of him, the story only said that an unknown man had been struck down in the same area by the blue light mystery. Beck was sure that he had seen this man before, though it was dark and he had only gotten a quick glance at him before Gray had acted. He had felt like this man was familiar to him and he was not going to leave Washington until he had investigated the matter and besides, he had another piece of business to attend to before his departure, he was set to have lunch that afternoon with his old friend and current Senator from California.

....

Kevin's bloodshot eyes burned as dawn approached. His search for ancient gold watches had yielded thousands of results–none useful. Auction listings, collector forums, even DIY goldsmithing tutorials cluttered his screen. He needed a scalpel, not a sledgehammer. Reaching into his digital toolbox, Kevin launched the filtering algorithm he'd coded junior year, the one that had earned him both detention and a perfect score at the state science fair. Now it would serve a higher purpose: penetrating the digital Fort Knox of government databases where the real secrets lay buried. These weren't ordinary websites, but labyrinthine systems of encrypted servers scattered across military installations nationwide. One wrong move navigating those defenses would land him in a windowless cell before his coffee went cold.

Jack's eyes snapped open, his mind still racing with thoughts of Carver's lecture, the gold watch, and his father's discovery about the man from Ulm. Rolling over in bed, he found himself thinking about his grandfather Simon–the brilliant young physics professor whose papers on interstellar travel had seemed so ahead of their time. Jack had devoured every word his grandfather had published before vanishing without explanation. The authorities had searched for weeks but found nothing except Simon's abandoned car beside that old mill in Maine. Jack's father George had grown up shadowed by this mystery, spending countless teenage afternoons at that mill, as though waiting for his father to step out of thin air and explain where he'd been all those years.

Jack clicked on the TV while pulling on his jeans, hoping to catch the

Boston College hockey score. The morning news droned through weather reports–another snowstorm coming–while he flipped through physics notes for his afternoon exam. A phrase cut through his distraction: "gold pocket watch" and "strange blue light." His head snapped up. The commercial break stretched endlessly before returning to a blonde reporter shivering outside the Museum of Science and Industry in D.C. Jack froze mid-motion when Harrison Carver's watch appeared on screen, now branded with a red "STOLEN" graphic. The reporter's voice tightened as she described how the mysterious blue light had nearly killed someone the night before the theft, then reappeared on security footage during the robbery itself.

Jack's legs went numb as the reporter's words sank in. The stolen watch. The mysterious blue light. A man hospitalized, found barely alive outside the museum. Coincidence? No way. Someone wanted that watch badly enough to risk everything. Carver's wild claims about its significance suddenly seemed less absurd. Jack grabbed his backpack and bolted from his room, his footsteps echoing down the dormitory hallway.

He knew exactly where to find Kevin–hunched over his keyboard, probably breaching security protocols that could land him in federal prison, the kind of digital trespassing that made Jack's palms sweat just thinking about it. Outside Kevin's door, Jack hesitated for only a second before knocking quickly and pushing the door open.

“You awake?” as Jack peered around the edge of the door.

“Yah, come in and shut the door,” Kevin said as he sat at his desk lit by the glow of two computer monitors.

“Have you been up all night? Man, this place looks like a garbage truck has rolled over and lost its load!” Jack said as he made his way through the maze of computer printouts and piles of laundry and the occasional pizza box and empty soda can.

“Sorry the housekeeper is on vacation,” Kevin said not looking away from the screen.

“Have you found anything interesting?” Jack asked as he cleared some books from a chair and sat down.

“It took me most of the night to get past the security and into the main frame system without tipping anyone off, but once I did, I was able to go pretty much anywhere I want.”

"Does that mean you have found something?"

"I have found everything about everything. You're right, there is not much mention of ancient gold watches in the mainstream, but when you get into the military's data base there are hundreds of mentions of these five gold watches."

"You hacked into the US military's computers?" Jack said shocked.

"Well not at first, I had to first hack into the CIA and use a pathway from their main frame into any computer system I wanted to from there," Kevin said in a matter-of-fact tone as if it were no big deal.

"You hacked into the CIA's computer? Are you out of your mind?" Jack said as he stood up to get a better look at what Kevin was doing. "What better computer system to hack, I mean the CIA is the place to start, what are they but an information gathering agency, they spy on everyone man, they even spy on each other. From their system I can go into just about any system in the world," Kevin added as he continued working at his computer.

"Do you think it is smart to be messing with the CIA? They don't take this kind of thing lightly and they will put you away for the rest of your days man," Jack said hoping that right this very moment the CIA wasn't about to kick down the door and take both of them away.

"You have little faith in me man, you don't think I know what I am doing but there is no way that they could possibly detect me," Kevin said with a hint of indignation in his voice.

"I have it set up as if my computer is actually part of the main frame of the CIA so when they see the main frame working, well that's all they see, there is no way to determine my computer from their own, it's a thing of beauty," Kevin beamed like a new father.

"I have no idea what you're talking about, but did you find anything or not?" Jack asked as he hoped that Kevin really did know what he was doing.

"As I said, there are hundreds of references to these five gold watches but nothing much about them; they come up in reports from different agents throughout the years, nothing of much interest just an agent here and there filing a report that mentioned different gold pocket watches and someone claiming they have special powers and stuff. But when you apply my genius creation to the search results you get something very interesting and that is when you really start finding out some strange stuff," Kevin told Jack proudly.

"What kind of interesting stuff, are these watches really from another planet, is that what you are saying?" Jack asked, his interest sparked by what Kevin had just told him.

"I don't know about these watches being from another planet, but what I do know is that they are real because some super-secret agency within our own government has spent over a billion dollars in search of these five watches since its creation shortly after the end of World War II. What is even more interesting is that it looks as if at one time or another at least one of the watches was in the hands of the Nazi's during World War II. They were able to use it to create some strange new kinds of weapons, only to have the watch stolen just as they were about to put the hammer down on the allies with these weapons," Kevin told Jack. He was really starting to think that this Mr. Carver from the other night had not been spinning a tale just to sound cool; he may have really found one of these elusive gold pocket watches.

What Kevin said about the watch being stolen during the Second World War reminded him about the theft of the gold watch in Washington. He told Kevin about the news report and about the strange blue lights that were found on two different surveillance systems.

"Man, this is really starting to get creepy, I don't know about aliens or not, but wow, this is all way more than I expected," Kevin said as he sat staring at Jack and thinking to himself about the fact that they were really on to something here and he felt it was something big.

"Can you find anything about the man who was almost killed the other night in front of the museum?" Jack asked.

"Probably, all I need to do is pull the news reports on the subject and also do a quick name search through the FBI and that should get us what we need," Kevin said as he rolled his chair over to another keyboard and began typing his search request in. After a few moments Kevin motioned for Jack to look at what he had found.

"You are not going to believe this man, but this Thomas guy who was found near death out in front of the museum had on him a gold pocket watch. There is nothing more, the only other things found on him were a small black case and an ID. It doesn't mention anything else and according to the police he has no known relatives," Kevin said in amazement as to how this thing was getting stranger and stranger by the second.

“What do you mean a gold pocket watch, is there a picture of the watch?” Jack asked as he read what Kevin had just pulled up on the screen.

“Not in the news report, but I would bet you a hundred bucks that the D.C. police have a photo of it, let me just take a peak in their main frame and see what we can dig up,” Kevin said as he went back to the keyboard and instructed the computer to search the records of the D.C. police.

“If they are on top of their job, they would have already put all this information into their computer and if they did that, then we can see everything they have on this guy, who, by the way, is still in the hospital at George Washington.

It took a few more minutes, but they were in luck, the police had in fact already entered the information along with all the photos into their database. Kevin worked at the keyboard and then sat back proud as to how quickly he had gotten to the information and even happier that they had done their part and put it into the system.

This detective Susan Young was on top of her job, she must be new, Kevin thought as he moved aside to let Jack look at the screen.

The watch looked much like any other gold pocket watch, Jack thought as he looked through the photos of the watch that was found on the man. His eyes scanned the other photos and then stopped on one, it took him a second because the quality of the photo was not the best, but it was a picture of the pocket watch with the outer face open and on the inside of the outer cover was a small picture, a cold shiver ran the length of his body.

“My God, it’s my grandfather!” Jack said in disbelief.

Chapter 22

Cambridge, Massachusetts
January 2001

Beck's hands trembled slightly as he held the newspaper. The grainy black and white photograph stared back at him–Thomas Grant, software engineer from Houston, Texas–the very man who had survived their attack outside the museum when the Cell Gun malfunctioned. Seeing Grant's face transported Beck back to Ulm, Germany in 1942, to their first fateful encounter with the man who had derailed decades of careful Deceiver planning.

Senator Buckley would be pleased. As one of the highest-ranking Deceivers in the U.S. government, Buckley had been waiting for a breakthrough like this.

"Senator Buckley will see you now, Mr. Beck," announced the receptionist with a practiced smile.

"Thank you," Beck replied, tucking the newspaper under his arm. He strode down the hallway toward Buckley's office, barely containing his excitement. After all these years, he'd located another of the five missing gold watches.

Beck leaned forward in his chair, eyes gleaming. "We're about to acquire a second gold watch, Senator," he said. "I've tracked down another one." He recounted the previous night's events at the museum–how he and Gray had nearly eliminated a man who seemed oddly familiar. "I've placed him now," Beck continued, tapping the newspaper. "This is the same man who, with his companion, sabotaged our operation and changed the course of the war. He stole the watch we were using to develop weapons technology for our German allies."

Beck smiled as Senator Buckley reached for the phone. This operation would be far simpler than the museum job–no breaking and entering, no confrontation, just bureaucratic efficiency. One call to their ally in the police department and the watch would be theirs. The Senator's fingers tapped the polished mahogany desk as he waited for the connection. "This is Senator Buckley for Commissioner Black," he said, voice smooth with the confidence of a man accustomed to immediate compliance.

Senator Buckley's voice boomed across the line. "Ed! How's life treating you at D.C. Police headquarters?" He paused, lowering his tone to a conspiratorial murmur. "I need a favor, but first–are you somewhere private?" After a moment, he nodded with satisfaction. "You've heard about that incident at the museum? The man they found unconscious? Well, I have reliable intelligence that he's carrying one of those gold watches we've discussed." His lips curled into a predatory smile as he leaned forward in his chair.

The Senator's voice dropped to a murmur before he placed the receiver back in its cradle. He swiveled toward Beck, the leather chair creaking beneath his substantial frame as he laced his fingers behind his head. "Commissioner Black is making the necessary arrangements," Buckley said, satisfaction evident in the slight curl of his lips. "He'll contact us momentarily."

....

It was only by chance that Thomas had the gold watch in his possession; he only had it because he had planned to meet and talk with Jack in Boston. Normally he would never have the watch; it had always been kept in a very safe location that he and only one other knew the location of.

Consciousness returned to Thomas slowly, like a tide washing in. The hospital room's dim lighting made his eyes ache, and each throb of his head brought back flashes of the museum attack. He'd been lucky to survive. He shifted against the stiff sheets, trying to piece together what had happened, when a sharp knock interrupted his thoughts. The door swung open to reveal a woman who couldn't have been more than in her mid-twenties, wearing a blazer that still had its store creases. Her dark ponytail was pulled so tight it seemed to lift her eyebrows, and a police badge caught the morning light filtering through the blinds.

"Mr. Grant," she said, pulling a small notebook from her pocket. "Detective Susan Young, D.C. Police. I'm glad to see you're recovering. Would you mind answering a few questions about the incident at the museum?"

Susan Young had just started her new position as detective with the D.C. police force, the gold shield still gleaming unnaturally bright against her navy blazer. She'd graduated at the top of her class of 300 at the academy in Maryland, where her marksmanship scores and investigative instincts had caught the attention of the Maryland State Police. They'd offered her a coveted position in their special investigation unit, where she'd spent a year analyzing crime scene evidence under fluorescent lights until her eyes burned. When the detective position opened at D.C. police, she'd submitted her application with trembling fingers, certain she'd be overlooked. The job offer had arrived on embossed department letterhead, shocking her into speechlessness.

Now, barely through her first week, with her desk still bearing nothing but a department-issue lamp and a single framed photo of her parents, Thomas's case had landed with a thud in her metal inbox–the museum assault relegated to local jurisdiction while men in dark suits from unnamed federal agencies had swooped in to handle the mysterious watch theft.

“I don’t mind,” Thomas said in a low whisper, his throat felt dry and there was a burnt taste in his mouth. “Would you like a glass of water Mr. Grant?” Susan asked as she reached for the jug to pour Thomas some water. Thomas nodded his head in agreement and took the glass of water, drank it down and then poured another. “Ok I will get started, and this should only take a few minutes,” Susan said as she opened her notebook and sifted through some papers.

“Do you remember what happened to you that night?” Susan asked as she looked at her notes. “I remember getting out of a taxi near the front of the Museum of Science and Industry and I noticed two men standing near the front steps. One of the men then turned and came at me, it all happened so fast, the last thing I remember was the attacker reached into his pocket and I remember a bright blue light and then everything went black,” Thomas said struggling to maintain his voice.

“Did you recognize any of the two men?” Susan asked.

Thomas shook his head no, all the while knowing he was lying and that in fact he knew one of the men, but there was no way he could tell the detective the truth.

Detective Young tapped her pen against her notebook. "Any theories about why these men targeted you, Mr. Grant?"

"None whatsoever," Thomas replied, reaching for his water glass again. The cool liquid soothed his parched throat.

"Disgruntled ex? Business rival with an axe to grind?" She scribbled something in her notebook without looking up.

Thomas shook his head. "I lead a rather uneventful life."

Detective Young snapped her notebook closed. "I'll let you rest, then." She turned to leave but paused. "One last thing–what brought you to the museum at that hour?"

"Just arrived from Boston." Thomas winced as he shifted position. "Flying makes me anxious. Thought a walk might help before heading to my hotel."

"Fair enough." She offered a professional smile. "Call if anything comes to mind." She reached into her purse and withdrew a plastic bag. "Your personal effects."

"Appreciate it," Thomas said, accepting the bag.

His fingers trembled slightly as he inventoried the contents–wallet, black case, and most importantly, the gold watch. Relief washed over him as he sank back against his pillow. Beck hadn't found it after all.

Chapter 23

Ulm, Germany
December 1942

Simon straightened his SS uniform, the black wool scratching against his neck as he summoned his most authoritative voice. "I am not concerned with your questions," he snapped, meeting Beck's suspicious gaze with cold blue eyes. "I am here to assess you and your progress. The Führer wants the weapon soon and sent me to make that happen."

Beck's thin lips tightened beneath his neatly trimmed mustache. "Leave us now," he ordered the guard and Thomas, his bony finger pointing toward the exit while his eyes remained fixed on Simon.

Thomas and the guard retreated up the worn concrete staircase, their footsteps echoing off the damp stone walls. Beck pivoted sharply on his polished boots and marched toward the center of the cavernous underground chamber. Simon followed, his heart pounding against his ribs.

The machine hovered ten feet above the floor–a metallic oval roughly the size of a small bus, its burnished silver surface reflecting the harsh fluorescent lights. No cables, no supports, nothing visible kept it suspended in the air. It emitted a low, pulsing hum that Simon could feel in his teeth.

Beck halted beside what appeared to be a hatch on the machine's underside and called upward in rapid German. Moments later, a man with wire-rimmed spectacles and oil-stained hands emerged, carefully descending a telescoping ladder that Beck had extended for him.

"This is Mr. Hofferstein," Beck announced, gesturing toward Simon with the same curt, dismissive tone. "He is here to be updated on our progress."

Beck's voice softened slightly. "What information do you require from us?"

He gestured toward the bespectacled man. "Mr. Gray and I are prepared to brief you thoroughly."

Simon's gaze remained fixed on the hovering metal oval. His mind raced with questions as he stared at the impossible machine suspended before him.

"Your timeline for completion?" Simon managed to ask, forcing his voice to remain steady.

"Two days, precisely as reported to the Führer," Beck replied sharply.

Simon struggled to formulate his next question. He needed information but had no context for what he was seeing.

"And its operational capabilities?" he ventured, having no real understanding of the machine's purpose.

Beck studied Simon's face with unnerving intensity. The seconds stretched painfully as Simon felt sweat forming beneath his collar. Beck's thin lips slowly curved upward.

"You truly have no concept of what you're looking at, do you?" Beck asked, his smile revealing teeth that seemed unnaturally sharp.

"No," Simon admitted, "I've never encountered anything like this."

Beck's lips peeled back to reveal those unnaturally pointed teeth. "I thought as much. No one has ever seen a machine like this–well, at least no one from this planet has." His voice dropped to a whisper that seemed to slither through the frigid air of the chamber. Simon fought the urge to step backward as Beck's pupils dilated until his eyes resembled black pools, reflecting the hovering machine's metallic sheen.

"This," Beck continued, running a pale, spidery hand along the craft's seamless hull, "is the Luftwaffe's salvation. When those Allied bombers come screaming across our skies, they'll encounter something beyond their comprehension." He gestured to six crystalline protrusions beneath the craft's belly. "These emit concentrated beams of light–pure energy–that can slice through steel as if it were butter. Six targets, six simultaneous kills." Beck tapped his knuckles against the hull, producing a sound like distant thunder. "And it draws power directly from the void between dimensions. No fuel. No limitations. It can outrun any aircraft on Earth by a factor of ten."

Simon's throat constricted as the implications crashed over him like a tidal wave. Two days. In two days, this otherworldly abomination would render the Allied air forces obsolete. The war–perhaps humanity itself–would be lost. But how could he possibly sabotage something he couldn't begin to understand?

While Simon faced Beck, Thomas prowled the labyrinthine corridors of the facility, his footsteps echoing against cold stone as he hunted for the gold pocket watch. The timepiece–with its intricate engravings and otherworldly mechanisms–had consumed his thoughts for weeks. Three days earlier, he'd nearly been discovered rifling through Beck's quarters–a spartan room with military-precise corners and the lingering scent of expensive cologne. His search had yielded nothing but suspicion. The watch, Thomas concluded, must never leave Beck's person, perhaps nestled in a hidden pocket of that immaculate uniform. What truly unsettled Thomas, sending a chill through his spine that had nothing to do with the facility's perpetual dampness, was the absence of other Deceivers. They operated like wolves–always in packs–their pale, too-perfect faces masking ancient malevolence. A solitary Deceiver was unprecedented, a deviation from patterns established over centuries of shadow war.

Thomas had meticulously crafted his persona as head of security for the Reich's "special projects," a position that granted him a leather-bound pass stamped with the eagle and swastika, opening doors throughout the Third Reich–except the ones that mattered most. The night before meeting Simon, Thomas had stood before those forbidden doors, studying their reinforced steel and the sophisticated locking mechanisms. Behind them lurked a Deceiver and undoubtedly a weapon of terrifying power. Even the black-uniformed SS guards, with their lightning bolt insignias and unquestioning loyalty, were forbidden entry. Thomas had spent weeks mapping patrol patterns, noting the rotation of guards, searching for any vulnerability in the impenetrable security that surrounded whatever unholy creation waited within.

A bitter wind howled through the deserted town square, driving snowflakes so thick they blurred the world into a white haze. Thomas hunched his shoulders against the gale, each gust slicing through his coat like a blade. Tonight, beneath that raging blizzard, he would risk everything. If he failed, Simon would remain lost and the Deceivers would march unchecked toward their grim vision of world domination. But the time for hesitation had passed; his carefully laid plan–days in the making–demanded action now, and the storm was the perfect cloak.

He slipped across the ice-slick cobblestones, boots crunching in the new drifts, until the tall red-brick façade of the old municipal building loomed at the square's edge. The snow cut visibility to only a few precarious steps, but Thomas pressed on, turning left to circle toward the west corner. From there he approached the makeshift guard post–

a rickety wooden lean-to that groaned under the weight of wind-driven snow.

Inside, a lone young sentinel trembled, shoulders hunched, breath steaming in the freezing air. Thomas stepped in and brushed the worst of the snow from his shoulders, his long overcoat releasing a faint puff of powdery crystals.

"Grueling night out there," he said, voice low, as he brushed snow from his sleeves and studied the guard's pale, chapped fingers.

The boy dared only a nod, teeth chattering as he gripped his rifle. Thomas had taken care to learn each man's name and weaknesses–the inexperienced were always posted to the coldest spots–and this one would be easy to persuade.

"Here," Thomas said, slipping off his leather gloves and pushing them toward the young guard. "Go inside for ten minutes. Get warm. I'll cover your post."

The guard's eyes widened. "Sir, I–my orders–"

"Consider me your relief," Thomas interrupted, voice steady despite the whipping wind. "I won't have any of my men freezing out here." At last, the guard surrendered, relief flooding his cheeks as he accepted the gloves. "Thank you, Sir," he murmured, hurrying into the main hallway, footsteps echoing off the brick walls.

Thomas watched him go, then settled into the shelter, drawing the rifle into his lap. The wind rattled the lean-to, but inside, he felt the calm focus of a man entirely committed. The night was at its fiercest–but so, too, was his resolve.

The guard's silhouette dissolved into the whiteout within seconds. Thomas counted to thirty, then abandoned his post, hunching against the wind as he navigated the fifty yards to the utility structure. His boots left tracks that the storm erased almost immediately. Days of reconnaissance had revealed this overlooked access point–a calculated risk, but the only viable path into a fortress designed to repel far more conventional infiltration attempts.

The small brick building contained the water main for the larger building and this is where the service tunnel was located, Thomas knew that there would be no guards in the tunnel because the only way in to the tunnel was from this building or the main building and both ends were secure or were until Thomas had sent the young guard inside to get warm. He had to hurry; he had no more than ten minutes to get inside and then get back out to the guard station.

The tunnel was small, just enough room for the water main and a man to make his way through, there were no lights in the tunnel, so Thomas used his small black case to light the way to the other end. It was about fifty yards to the end of the tunnel where it entered the main building, from what Thomas was able to determine the tunnel would end and allow him to enter the main building without being seen.

He made his way to the end where the tunnel entered the building and there in front of him was a small steel door and a metal ladder that went up some twenty feet, he climbed the ladder to the top where was able to get a view of the entire main building.

Thomas stayed as long as he dared and took in everything he could; he did not want to risk taking any photos with his black instrument, so he just spent his time trying to commit what he was seeing to memory. Thomas was able to catch a glimpse of only one man and right away he knew who this man was, he had seen him before in the local tavern, it was Herr Beck, but that was only one of many names this man must have had over the years. Herr Beck was a Deceiver, and right there in his hands was a gold pocket watch and he was using it to gain information that very instant.

Thomas could wait no longer, though he wanted to stay and watch this man, he knew that the young SS guard would soon be returning and he must get back before he did or he would be found out and any chance to stop the Deceivers and capture the gold pocket watch would be lost forever.

Thomas had just made it back to the shelter moments before the SS guard returned to his post.

“Thank you, Sir,” the young guard said to Thomas as he entered the shelter to reclaim his post.

“My pleasure” Thomas said with a nod, “I trust you got some warmth,” Thomas said trying to act as if nothing important were going on, all the while his mind was still focused on the image of the gold watch he had just seen.

“Yes Sir, again thank you,” The young guard said to Thomas.

“Well, I think I will go enjoy some of the warmth myself,” Thomas said as he pulled his overcoat tight and exited the shelter. “Have a good night," Thomas said over his shoulder as he stepped back into the full force of the storm.

Simon was still with Beck and Gray as Thomas made his way over to the house where Beck was staying alone. He had never seen Beck with anyone for more than a few moments and was still puzzled as to why there did not appear to be any other Deceivers near, he knew that Beck had in his possession a gold pocket watch and that would account for the advanced technology being developed here in Ulm, but where were the other Deceivers and how come he hasn't been able to find them?

Thomas wanted to take this opportunity to get back inside the house where Beck was staying to see if he could find anything more out about where the watch was being kept, though he fully suspected that the watch never left the Becks possession, as Beck knew just how valuable the watch was. Thomas entered without any problem and began to search the house; he had been here before but was not able to search the entire house before he had to leave. He made his way up the staircase and into Becks' room; Thomas looked around the room and went over to a small chest that sat on the night table near the bed. The chest wasn't large, about the size of an envelope and had writing on it that would be unreadable for anyone not from the same planet as Beck was.

Thomas had found what he was after, there was piece of paper and on it a list of names of the other Deceivers and their current positions around the world. The writing was the same as the writing on the outside of the small chest. There were hundreds of names on the paper, so Thomas took out his small black case, moved his finger around the front of it and then pressed the face of it to the paper and moved it slowly down the paper allowing it to make an exact image of the information contained on it. Thomas, not wanting to risk discovery, left the house and returned to the large brick building.

Simon spent the entire day with Beck and Gray, he found out that the machine would be impervious to any conventional weapon that the Allies had in their arsenal and that the only way to destroy this machine was to destroy the power supply from within however you needed a special tool to open the door and only Beck and Gray knew what that tool was and how to use it. Beck's arrogance was palpable as he revealed detail after detail about the machine. Simon merely had to pose a question, and Beck would launch into an elaborate explanation, his eyes gleaming with self-satisfaction.

He even divulged the Nazis' plans for the weapon's maiden

deployment, seemingly oblivious to how much intelligence he was surrendering to a virtual stranger.

Simon almost gave out a laugh when he asked Beck who had come up with such an amazing machine and Beck answered that it was his creation. Simon knew full well that Beck was using a gold pocket watch to obtain this sort of technology and had to hold back his amusement toward Beck and his large ego. "Well Mr. Beck your work is very impressive and sounds like the war may be over quite soon," Simon said to Beck wanting to feed Beck's ego just a bit more, he could hardly wait until he saw the look on Beck's face when his machine was destroyed and his source of knowledge stolen from him.

"Are there any further questions Mr. Hofferstein?" Beck asked Simon as he began to walk in the direction of the two doors that they had entered through.

"No, thank you for your time, all of this is quite amazing," Simon said as he followed behind Beck in the direction of the doors. "I will return to Berlin and brief the Fuhrer on the progress of your project, I am sure he will be very pleased," Simon said to Beck as the neared the door.

Simon made his way back up the staircase to the room with the red-faced guard and inquired to the location of Thomas. The portly faced man informed Simon that he was waiting for him at the tavern across the square near the inn they had stayed at the previous night. Simon thanked the guard and left.

As Simon walked across the square in the direction of the tavern, he noticed the weather was warming a bit and the wind had changed direction from the north to out of the west. The tavern was nearly empty, so it took Simon only a moment to locate Thomas sitting in a corner. He appeared to be reading from a paper he held in his hand and only noticed Simon when he arrived at the table where he was sitting.

"Did everything go well?" Thomas asked as he placed the paper face down on the table in front of Simon. "Yes, Beck told me all about the machine, he seemed to enjoy telling me. I think it fed his already sizable ego," Simon said to Thomas

"Good. Let us have a bite to eat and discuss the plan that we talked about last night," Thomas said as he motioned for the waiter.

Thomas's eyes scanned the freshly transferred information, his small black case now tucked away. Unbeknownst to him, crucial details about their precarious situation remained several pages ahead. Meanwhile, across town, Beck stood at his telephone, speaking rapid German into the receiver. His words traveled through the wire to Berlin, setting in motion events that could soon jeopardize not only their mission but their very lives.

Chapter 24

Cambridge, Massachusetts
January 2001

Kevin's jaw dropped. "Wait, what did you just say?" Jack leaned closer to the screen, his finger trembling slightly as he pointed. "The man on the left–that's my grandfather." "Your grandfather?" Kevin's voice rose as he tapped the monitor with his fingernail. "This guy right here? The one standing next to Thomas Grant?"

“Can you print this?” Jack asked still staring at the screen.

“Sure, no problem,” Kevin said as he stood up to turn on the printer. “I can’t believe this man,” Kevin added as he instructed the printer to print.

The printer came to life and a few seconds later Jack was holding a photo of his grandfather, his mind was all over the place, he didn’t know if he should call his father about what he had found, or if he should try and keep looking for more. Jack stood there holding the paper in silence for a moment and gathered his thoughts.

“We need to find out who this man in the picture with my grandfather is,” Jack said as he sat back down.

“Well, we already know the man’s name, its right here his name is Thomas Grant, he is some sort of computer software guy from Houston,” Kevin said wondering what more they could get on the man.

“How does this guy know my grandfather and how does he have a picture of my grandfather that was clearly taken after he went missing?” Jack asked as he tried to put all of the pieces together in his mind. He was missing something but just couldn’t put his finger on what it was.

“The FBI doesn’t have anything more on this guy,” Kevin said as he looked at Jack

“Wait! Put up the picture from the paper a few days ago and then put up the one from the D.C. police,” Jack said in a hurry, hoping his hunch was correct.

Kevin went back to the keyboard and made both pictures appear side by side on the screen, and there it was right in front of both of them.

“Oh wow man, what the heck is going on here?” Kevin said as he stared at the screen. “This Thomas guy looks the same age now as he does in the picture with your grandfather.”

Jack stared at the two images of Thomas Grant side by side on the screen. Despite the decades that should have separated them, the man's face hadn't aged a day. In the older photograph with his grandfather, Thomas wore a high-waisted suit with wide lapels straight out of the post-war era. The newspaper photo showed the same unlined face, now framed by a modern haircut and dressed in a contemporary button-down shirt. The contradiction made Jack's pulse quicken–these photos spanned generations, yet Thomas Grant remained frozen in time.

“How can we find out more on this guy?” Jack asked as he looked over to Kevin, knowing that his friend would find a way to keep on digging.

Kevin shook his head, fingers still flying across the keyboard. "Man, it's weird. No FBI records, nothing in CIA databases. I've tried birth certificates, school records, DMV–zip. It's like this Thomas Grant materialized out of nowhere in his forties with a complete identity but zero history."

Jack leaned forward, tapping the edge of the desk. "What about regular internet searches? News archives, social media, anything that might not be in government systems?"

Kevin shook his head. "I doubt we'll get anywhere with a name search. If this guy's been using aliases, we'd just be wasting our time."

They fell silent. Jack drummed his fingers on the desk, the frustration building inside him. After all these years without a single lead about his grandfather's disappearance, he finally had something tangible–a photograph–and now they were hitting wall after wall. He couldn't let the trail go cold.

Jack checked his watch. His father would be lecturing now and wouldn't be free until after lunch. How exactly do you tell someone you've found a picture of their long-missing father? This wasn't news for a phone call. He needed to fly to Bangor and show his father the evidence in person.

"What if we tried something else?" Kevin suddenly perked up. "We could call the hospital where Thomas is staying, see if they'd let us talk to him."

Jack considered this. "The article said he was near death. He might not be able to speak." He paused, reconsidering. "But you know what? It's worth a shot."

“What could it hurt?” Kevin asked.

Jack leaned forward, eyes bright with determination. "What have we got to lose? Let's do it."

Kevin nodded, already punching the number for George Washington Hospital into his phone. The line clicked after three rings.

"George Washington University Hospital, how may I direct your call?" a woman's voice answered.

"I'd like to speak with a patient–Thomas Grant," Kevin said, giving Jack a thumbs-up.

The operator paused. "I'm sorry, sir. Mr. Grant was discharged early this morning."

Kevin's face fell as he ended the call. "So much for 'near death.' Our mystery man walked out of there hours ago."

“Do you think that he is headed back to Houston?” Jack asked. “Maybe we can reach him there?”

“Let me see what I can find out, give me a second,” Kevin said as he spun around in his chair and began working at the computer again.

After a few minutes of searching Kevin was even more puzzled as to what he was finding. “Hey man, you won’t believe this but the address and phone number on Grant’s ID is a hardware store, it’s not even a house. The more we dig into this guy the stranger it gets,” Kevin said as he shook his head in frustration.

While Kevin was trying to find out how to reach Thomas using the information on his ID, Jack was still trying to put all the pieces together, he kept turning his attention to the watch; the watch was at the root of all of this but how? There had been a gold pocket watch taken from the museum, the very watch that Mr. Carver had claimed was made by the hands of aliens. Then there was the mention of the five gold pocket watches that his father had told him about the night before, and finally this man Thomas Grant was found with a gold pocket watch with a silver key attached to the end of the gold chain.

Jack kept trying to put everything in order in his mind; obviously there was something to these watches, but he wasn't sure what that was just yet.

It took a minute for Jack to see the whole picture, but when he did, he knew he was on to something and needed to see his grandmother as soon as he could.

"Get packed, we are going to Maine," Jack said as he stood up from his chair.

"What, when?" Kevin asked.

"Right now, I need to see my grandmother about something, and it can't wait. Just hurry up, I will fill you in on the plane and bring your laptop, we may need it," Jack said as he shot out the door and down the hall to his room.

It was the gold pocket watch, if his memory was correct, the gold pocket watch that his grandfather used to carry was the same one that Thomas Grant had on him in Washington D.C.

Chapter 25

Washington, D.C.
January 2001

D.C. Police Commissioner Black quickly hung up the phone, 'damn it' he thought to himself, he didn't want to call Senator Buckley and tell him that the watch was given back to this Mr. Grant who had already left the hospital, but he knew that he had to make the call and deliver the bad news no matter the reaction of the Senator.

Senator Buckley did not like to hear bad news; he had spent more than three hundred years as the leader of the Deceivers only to have the Protectors foil his plans time and again. Beck had just informed him that Thomas Grant, along with his companion, had been the ones who had ruined his plan for world domination during World War II. They were the ones who had infiltrated their secret project in Ulm Germany and were able to destroy the flying weapon and steal the gold watch and with it their ability to create and use their advanced weapons to crush the allies and take their rightful position as the leaders of this planet.

Senator Buckley had been In the United States Senate for twenty years now and was becoming more powerful by the year. He had his sights set on a much higher office and when he obtained it, he would be able to finish his plan of world domination. As the current leader of the Deceivers it was Buckley's responsibility to gain positions of power so he could bring the full influence of the Deceivers upon man, since they had not had possession of a gold watch since the end of the 1950's when the watch they had been using to rapidly advance the technology of the USSR was taken and lost to them. Buckley had been setting the plan in place for the day they would again have the use of one of the gold pocket watches and now that they had one in their possession and soon to have a second, it was now time to begin to put the final pieces of the plan into motion.

Beck was enroute to Commissioner Black's office, he wanted to be present when the commissioner had retrieved the watch, when his cell phone rang.

"Beck here," he said in his normal business-like tone.

"Get back here, they don't have it anymore and he has left the hospital," Senator Buckley said the frustration clearly evident to Beck.

"I know, I was with Black when he called the detective who was handling the case and she told him she had given his things back to him this morning after speaking with him. I went to the hospital with the commissioner to retrieve the watch and we found out that he was already gone," Beck explained to Senator Buckley. "I am on my way back now," Beck said as he ended the call and instructed the cab driver to take him back to the Capital.

Detective Susan Young drummed her fingers on her desk, replaying the conversation with Police Commissioner Black. Something was off. The Commissioner had called specifically about Grant's gold pocket watch, and when she'd mentioned returning it to its owner that morning, his tone had shifted abruptly. The urgency in his voice before he hung up left her unsettled. Since when did the city's top cop concern himself with a tourist's personal effects? And why had the mention of the watch's return prompted such a hasty end to their call?

She had the feeling when she was talking to Mr. Grant that he wasn't telling her everything about what had happened to him that night in front of the museum, but there was no reason to press the issue, that was until the strange phone call she just received from the commissioner. She left her desk and headed to the hospital to have another conversation with Mr. Grant.

Susan arrived at the hospital ten minutes later and found that Mr. Grant had checked himself out of the hospital not long after she had spoken with him that morning.

"He said he wanted to get home and insisted on checking himself out of the hospital right then, the doctors tried to convince him to stay another day for observation and he flatly refused saying he had to get home," the tall dark-haired nurse explained to Susan.

"He just said he had to get home, that's all, why is he in trouble or something?" the nurse asked looking concerned.

"No, I just had a few more questions for him; I didn't think he was in any position to leave with the way he looked this morning." Susan added as the strangeness of all this started to seem a bit off.

"Oh, I thought he might be, since the Police Commissioner himself had just wanted to see Mr. Grant," the nurse added as she started to walk off.

"Wait, you mean the Police Commissioner came here to see Mr. Grant?" Susan said wanting to make sure she had heard right but already knowing she had.

“Yes, he and another man came by and wanted to speak with him and when I said they couldn’t he told me he was the D.C. Police Commissioner and he wanted to speak with Mr. Grant immediately. When I told him that Mr. Grant had checked out he and the other man just turned and left quickly,” the nurse said.

“Who was the other man that was with him?” Susan asked, curious as to why the police commissioner would be so interested in this case as to come down here and talk to Mr. Grant.

“I don’t know, he didn’t speak,”

“Was he in a police uniform?”

“No, he was dressed in a very nice suit.”

“Ok thank you for your time,” Susan said to the nurse as she turned to leave the hospital, very curious as to all of the events surrounding Mr. Grant

Before Susan left the hospital, she had an idea that she wanted to check out. Susan headed down the main hall to the main entrance and walked up to the information desk.

“I am Detective Susan Young, and I need to speak with the hospital’s head of security,” Susan said as she showed the elderly woman her police identification.

“One moment ma’am, I will see if I can reach him for you,” the woman said as she picked up the phone. “He will be here in a moment, you can wait over there,” the elderly woman said as she motioned to a small sitting area.

“Thank you,” Susan said as she smiled at the woman and went to wait for the security officer.

Something was going on, she didn’t know what it was, but she had made up her mind that she would find out what it was.

Chapter 26

Washington, D.C.
January 2001

The news report flickered across the television screen in Thomas's hospital room–a gold pocket watch stolen from the museum. His pulse quickened. He knew exactly who had taken it, and they would come for him next. He couldn't risk being found before reaching Jack Douglas.

Hours later at the airport, Thomas's ribs still ached with each breath, a reminder of how narrowly he'd escaped death. Boston couldn't wait. With a gold watch now in the Deceivers' possession, their plans would accelerate rapidly. Jack's involvement was no longer optional–it had become necessary. Thomas only hoped the young man could accept the truth about his family's extraordinary heritage.

Thomas gripped the armrests of his narrow seat as the plane banked sharply to the left, his knuckles whitening with each pocket of turbulence. The recycled cabin air tasted stale in his mouth. He tried focusing on the speech he'd rehearsed a dozen times–how to tell Jack Douglas about Simon's brilliant mind, about William's courage during the war, about the legacy hidden in their DNA. The words to explain alien heritage to a twenty-year-old college student seemed inadequate no matter how he arranged them. When the wheels finally screeched against the Boston tarmac, Thomas exhaled a breath he hadn't realized he was holding. These fragile aluminum tubes humans hurled through the sky were miracles of ingenuity, yet dangerously primitive by Protector standards. "Where to?" asked the cab driver, a heavyset man with three days of stubble, as Thomas settled into the cracked leather backseat that smelled faintly of cigarettes and pine air freshener. “Harvard Campus please,” Thomas said as he sat back for the ride across town.

It took longer than normal to reach the campus due to the rush hour traffic but that gave Thomas time to formulate his plan on how to best approach Jack Douglas. The car pulled up to a large wrought iron gate near Harvard Square, Thomas paid the driver and exited the cab, his energy fading fast. The effects of the blast had still not worn off, and Thomas knew that they wouldn't for at least a few more days. He recognized the weapon that nearly killed him, but what puzzled him more was how the Deceivers were able to have it in their possession, however, finding out how the Deceivers obtained the weapon from

Allan Knight would have to wait until the matter at hand had been dealt with.

The weather had not changed much since Thomas departed a few days ago, the snow had let up to just a few flurries, but the wind blew into him with a renewed icy blast that forced him to pull his overcoat tight around his body in a vain effort to block out the chill he was starting to feel.

Thomas walked slowly through the campus as his body complained with each step he took. He turned and made his way to the dorm where Jack lived and hoped that he would find him there and if not, he would wait for him to return. Thomas made his way down the warm hallway; no one even paid much attention to him as he moved in the direction of Jacks dorm room. Thomas had mastered looking like he belonged and therefore he didn't draw any undue attention to himself when moving about among different people. He walked up to Jack's door and without any hesitation knocked firmly and waited, hoping that Jack would be inside. Another knock did not produce results so Thomas determined that Jack was out, perhaps at dinner or at his hockey practice when a passing student stopped to talk to Thomas.

"If you're looking for Jack he and Kevin went home for a few days," the young man said as he stood near Thomas.

"He went home?" Thomas repeated out loud. "Yeah, they left today," the boy said as he started on his way down the hall.

"Ok, Thanks for your help".

"No problem, have a good one".

Home. The word echoed in Thomas's mind as he stood alone in the hallway. A mid-week departure with Kevin in tow seemed suspicious at best, alarming at worst. After a moment's deliberation, Thomas surveyed the empty corridor, then extracted a small black case from his pocket. He positioned it against Jack's door lock, tracing his finger across its surface until a soft click signaled success. The door swung open, and Thomas slipped inside. If something had driven Jack to leave campus so abruptly, the evidence might be waiting here.

There was not much in the room that gave any clues as to what would have caused the sudden departure of the two boys. Thomas sat in the room, pulled the small black case from his pocket and proceeded to search for any information as to whether there had been a family emergency that would explain the departure, but nothing could be found. Thomas sat in Jack's desk chair and thought about his next move, should he go to Maine on the next possible flight, or should he wait here for Jack to return, but how long would that be? The more time that passed by without Jack being told of the situation, the more likely he may not ever know if Beck and the Deceivers ever caught up to him before he could get to Jack.

Thomas got up and left the room. He headed back out into the cold and back to the airport, things were not going as planned. He had not expected to find Beck at Carvers lecture the other night and had not expected to meet up with him again in front of the museum and nearly get killed, then to have Jack suddenly leave school and head home just as he had come back to tell him the truth about who he was and what was going on with the struggle against the Deceivers.

Back outside in the cold wind Thomas headed in the direction of Harvard Square to catch a cab ride to the airport. As he sat in the rear of the cab his thoughts began to drift back to his days with Simon in Ulm Germany, how Simon had saved his life and they were able to put a stop to the Deceivers and the Nazi war machine.

Chapter 27

Ulm, Germany
December 1942

The small tavern's wooden beams sagged with age; its windows fogged with decades of pipe smoke. Thomas and Simon hunched over their plates of boiled potatoes and sausage, the din of clinking glasses and murmured German conversations providing cover for their silence. Across the cobblestone town square loomed the imposing red brick Gestapo headquarters, its Nazi flag hanging limp in the evening air. Simon's fork scraped against his plate as he noticed a yellowed paper lying face down beside Thomas's half-empty stein.

"What is that?" Simon whispered, his American accent carefully masked as he nodded toward the document.

Thomas's weathered face tensed. His eyes, constantly scanning the room for eavesdroppers, briefly met Simon's before returning to the paper. "Something I discovered while you were occupied with Beck," he murmured, his voice barely audible above the tavern's ambient noise.

"What does it say?"

"Haven't had the chance to examine it properly. Your arrival interrupted my first look." Thomas dabbed his mouth with a frayed napkin. "We'll discuss it later, somewhere secure."

"Understood," Simon replied, returning to his cooling meal.

"Remember our rendezvous arrangements," Thomas cautioned as he pushed back his chair, its legs scraping against the uneven floorboards. He folded the paper with practiced precision before tucking it into his worn leather jacket.

As Thomas disappeared through the tavern's heavy oak door, Simon stared into his plate, his appetite gone. His mind drifted to his home in Maine–to five-year-old George's gap-toothed smile and Rebecca's flowing chestnut hair. The weight of their uncertainty crushed him more than any Nazi threat. Would they recognize him if–when–he returned?

Thomas stepped into the crisp night air, his breath forming clouds as he hurried across the square toward the half-timbered Inn. The paper from Beck's study seemed to burn in his pocket. Inside the dimly lit lobby, Herr Walker's gaunt face appeared from behind the reception desk, his eyes darting nervously as he approached.

Herr Walker's gaunt face twitched as he approached Thomas. "Herr Grant, forgive me," he said, his voice barely above a whisper, "but you have a message from a Herr Beck to return immediately to the office." His yellowed fingers fidgeted with his worn lapel as his rheumy eyes darted around the wood-paneled lobby, scanning the shadows between the heavy burgundy drapes.

"He also requests that you bring back your companion, a Mr. Hofferstein, with you." A bead of sweat trickled down Walker's temple despite the chill that seeped through the ancient stone walls.

Thomas's jaw tightened beneath his three-day stubble. His mind raced through possibilities like a card dealer shuffling a deck. Beck's invitation could be innocent–or a trap closing around them like a steel jaw.

"Thank you, Herr Walker," Thomas replied, his German accent flawless, "however I do not know where Mr. Hofferstein is at the moment, but I will relay the message to him as soon as I see him." He maintained steady eye contact, willing the innkeeper to accept his lie.

Walker leaned closer, the scent of schnapps and fear on his breath. I have been instructed to call Mr. Beck as soon as you came back," he whispered, his voice trembling like autumn leaves. "I am not supposed to tell you that some SS guards have already been in your rooms. They left everything... disturbed."

"I am sure I do not know what this is all about," Thomas responded, his face a mask of practiced confusion while his pulse hammered against his collar. The folded paper seemed to burn against his chest. Whatever Beck had discovered, it meant they were marked men now.

Thomas thought for a moment, he and Simon were indeed in a great deal of danger, but Herr Walker had told him something he was instructed not to tell him, maybe, just maybe Herr Walker was willing to help. Thomas saw no other option in the current situation, so he decided to risk enlisting Herr Walker's help.

“Herr Walker do you have a pen that I might use for a moment?” Thomas asked calmly. Herr Walker paused and looked about the lobby, no one was in sight at the moment, but he knew that if Mr. Grant and his companion did not report to Beck very soon that there would be SS guards swarming the town in search of them and that anyone who helped the two in any way would be shot and who knows what would happen to their families.

“Yes of course, why don’t you come to my office I think there is one there you may use,” Herr Walker said as he again scanned the lobby.

The blue tip of a fountain pen peeked from Herr Walker's shirt pocket. Thomas caught the glint of it under the lobby's dim light and understood immediately–this man was risking everything to help them. Without a word, they slipped into the rear office where Walker locked the door with trembling fingers.

"Beck's invitation is a death sentence," Walker whispered, his voice barely disturbing the air between them. Thomas squeezed the innkeeper's bony shoulder. "I won't drag you into this."

He withdrew a scrap of paper, his handwriting urgent and cramped as he scribbled across it. "But Simon–he's still at the tavern. We're meant to meet in an hour. If he walks into their trap..."

Walker pocketed the note with a decisive nod. "I'll see he gets this. Now you must disappear."

The innkeeper pressed against a section of wainscoting, revealing a second door. "This way," he urged, guiding Thomas down a narrow corridor so tight their shoulders brushed the walls. "I know somewhere they won't think to look."

Walker's voice dropped to a whisper. "This passage connects to the tavern, but midway there's a hiding place my brother and I built before Hitler's shadow fell across our town."

His fingers traced the wall's contours until something clicked beneath the plaster. A panel swung inward on silent hinges. Thomas peered into a cramped chamber barely ten feet square. A military cot was pushed against one wall, while shelves of tinned rations and chipped porcelain lined another.

"It isn't much," Walker murmured, stepping aside with a slight bow. "But it will keep you beyond their reach–for now."

Chapter 28

Ulm, Germany
December 1942

Herr Walker's weathered face creased with urgency. "You stay here; I will go to my brother at the Tavern and make sure your companion gets this note." He stepped back into the narrow hallway, his broad shoulders nearly touching both walls, and slid the wooden panel back into place with a hollow thud.

Thomas listened as Herr Walker's heavy footsteps faded into silence. The secret room was claustrophobic–barely eight feet square with crumbling plaster walls stained yellow from decades of cigarette smoke. A single dusty bulb dangled from a frayed wire, casting harsh shadows across the room's sparse furnishings: a metal cot with a thin, striped mattress and a three-legged stool. Thomas ran his fingers through his sweat-dampened hair, praying Herr Walker would reach Simon before the black-uniformed SS and the calculating Beck did. Beck had discovered something crucial, though what information he'd uncovered and how remained a mystery. Thomas's fingers brushed against the folded paper in his pocket. He pulled it out, the crisp edges softened by nervous handling, and lowered himself onto the creaking cot to read.

Meanwhile, Herr Walker navigated the dank underground passage, the earthen floor cool beneath his hurried steps. The tunnel, a relic dating back to medieval times, emerged behind a false pantry shelf just outside the tavern's steamy kitchen. From this vantage point, he spotted Simon sitting alone at a corner table, nursing a half-empty stein of amber beer. Walker moved swiftly toward his brother, who stood behind the polished oak bar, methodically drying glasses with a white cloth and whistling a melancholy folk tune from their Bavarian childhood. The innkeeper's sudden appearance startled his brother, whose ruddy face registered surprise before leaning in to hear the whispered news. Simon observed the brothers' furtive conversation, noting their repeated glances in his direction. A knot formed in his stomach as the innkeeper–whom Simon recognized as the proprietor of the small guesthouse where he and Thomas had spent the previous night–approached his table with measured steps, his expression grave beneath his salt-and-pepper mustache.

Herr Walker approached the table and slid a folded piece of paper across the worn surface. "From Mr. Grant," he said quietly, his voice barely audible over the tavern's ambient noise.

Simon's fingers hovered above the paper. He studied the man's face, searching for any sign of deception. Walker's eyes darted repeatedly toward the entrance, his jaw tense beneath his mustache. Simon unfolded the note with deliberate care. Five words in Thomas's hurried scrawl made his blood run cold: "Get out now. We're compromised!"

A flood of thoughts raced through Simon's mind all at once, they had been discovered, but how? Beck didn't suspect a thing Simon was sure of it, what was Thomas talking about, how could they stop now, and how was he supposed to get out by himself?

"Where is Mr. Grant now?" Simon asked as he placed the paper in his pocket.

Herr Walker hesitated for a moment and again looked at the door, just before he spoke Simon heard the bartender say something quickly to the man at his table. Before the man could respond the door to the tavern opened and in rushed two SS guards.

The guards immediately walked up to Simon's table and stopped; they then demanded that he stand as they pointed their automatic weapons at him. "May I help you?" Simon tried to ask in a casual voice. "Come with us. Mr. Beck would like to speak with you," The taller of the two guards barked in a very harsh tone.

"Well, you can have Mr. Beck join me here for a bite," Simon responded as if all of this were very natural.

"GET UP NOW!!" The tall guard said again, this time bringing the tip of his weapon closer to Simon's face.

"Ok, ok no need to get angry about all of this," Simon said as he slid back his chair and stood, he noticed that the man who handed him the note had left and he thought to himself that he didn't blame him for doing so.

Simon stood and the smaller guard walked up and placed his gun barrel into Simons back and instructed him to walk as he gave a sharp push with his weapon. Simon was still trying to find a way out of his current situation when chaos erupted in the tavern. Suddenly out of nowhere a man came flying into the fray and knocked over the smaller guard that had been pushing Simon along. Before Simon could turn to see what was going on he was knocked to the floor and then suddenly a bright flash filled the room and one of the guards fell to the floor next to him. Then another bright flash sent the taller guard hurling into the wall across the room where he slumped to the floor.

Chapter 29

Cambridge, Massachusetts
January 2001

Kevin buckled his seatbelt and frowned at Jack. "What exactly was so urgent we had to bail on everything and rush back to Bangor?"

Jack pulled the photograph from his pocket, tapping his finger against a thin gold chain visible across his grandfather's vest. "See that? My grandfather always carried a gold pocket watch. Always."

"Let me guess." Kevin's eyebrows arched skeptically. "You think it's one of the five missing watches from this whole conspiracy theory?"

"I honestly don't know." Jack tucked the photo away as the engines roared and the plane lifted off, banking northward toward Maine. "But you can't deny it's weird–my grandfather's picture inside that stranger's watch, plus everything about Carver's stolen timepiece. It's all connected somehow."

Kevin pressed his forehead against the window, watching the ground fall away. "Fair enough. The deeper we go, the weirder this gets." His knuckles whitened against the armrest as turbulence rattled the cabin.

Jack and Kevin sat in silence for a few minutes as the plane made its way north to Bangor. Jack was thinking about this guy from Germany that talked about the gold pocket watches and the struggle between good aliens and bad aliens. Maybe there was something to his claims after all; his father sure seemed interested in what this guy had to say.

Jack nudged Kevin with his elbow. "When we get to my parent's house I need you to find out everything you can on the guy from Germany who claims he has proof of this battle between these good and bad aliens during the war," Jacks said as he made a few notes on some paper to remind him to call his coach and let him know he would be missing practice tonight.

"We don't need to wait until we get there," Kevin said as he reached into his computer bag and pulled out a stack of papers. "I printed a bunch of stuff from the guy's website last night; we were so busy talking about this Grant guy I forget to show them to you," Kevin added as he handed the papers to Jack.

"What's in them?" Jack asked as he looked and the sheets of papers.

"I don't know, I didn't have time to read them last night, so I just told the computer to print everything from his site, I haven't even looked at them," Kevin said as he shifted in his seat. "You read them, I am going to grab some sleep, I have been up all night, remember?" He added as he put his head back and shut his eyes.

Jack began to scan through the papers that were in no particular order. There were claims that there had been this age-old battle between these so-called good Aliens' and the other aliens called 'the Deceivers'. According to this guy Walker, who lived in Ulm Germany, his grandfather had met two of the 'good Aliens' during the war and helped them defeat the Nazis and destroy some sort of secret weapon that the bad Aliens were working on to use against the allies and help the Nazis take over the world.

Jack thought to himself that this guy was indeed way out there with his claims, no wonder why he had been labeled a crackpot by the mainstream. Jack skipped through to some photos that Walker claimed were of the two good Aliens that his grandfather had helped destroy some weapon that was to be used against the allies, some sort of super weapon of sorts. He was scanning the photos on the printouts, they were not the best quality and some of the detail was hard to make out, but right there in front of him was a photo of his grandfather and Mr. Grant, it was the same picture that was in the watch found on Mr. Grant.

Jack sat there just staring at the photo with the words good aliens running over and over in his mind, this Walker was calling his grandfather a "good alien", none of this made any sense to Jack, how did this man from Ulm Germany have a photo of his grandfather who had disappeared, never to be seen again? Jack noticed the small caption just below the photo, the date said December 1942, at least that's what he thought it said, his reading of German was a bit sketchy at best.

"Take a look at this." Jack said as he nudged Kevin with his elbow.

"Sleeping here, can't it wait until we land?" Kevin asked as he tried to ignore Jack.

"Just look at this you can sleep later," Jack said as he thrust the paper with the photo into Kevin's lap.

"Fine, I will look, who needs sleep?" Kevin said grumpily as he grabbed the paper and looked at the pictures.

"What the hell?" Kevin said as he realized what he was looking at. "Is this the same as the one found in the watch?" he asked.

"Yes, the same photo, and take a look at the date, December 1942, that's the very same month...."

"Yes, I know that's the very same month your grandfather disappeared," Kevin interrupted, still amazed at what he was looking at.

"Man, I don't have to tell you, but there are some strange things going on here. How could this Walker guy have a picture of your grandfather and Mr. Grant?" Kevin asked as he felt a chill run down his back.

"My guess is that it was his grandfather who took the photo in the first place," Jack added as he again looked at the picture.

"You know what is strange, if this picture is really from 1942 like you say, then how do you explain this picture?" Kevin asked as he held up a photo he had printed of Mr. Grant that had been in the paper of few days back.

"What do you mean?" Jack asked not quite sure what Kevin was getting at.

"Look man, this guy looks the same age now as he did then, how can that be?" he said shaking his head.

"I don't know what to think," Jack said not wanting to bring up the fact just yet, that this Mr. Walker had labeled his grandfather as an alien.

"All I know is that I want to find out what really happened to my grandfather," Jack said as he looked over to Kevin.

"Me too, me too," Kevin said as he looked down once again at the picture.

The Captain came over the intercom and announced that they were on final approach and to prepare for landing. Jack stared forward thinking of everything he and Kevin had uncovered in the past few days and how he was going to tell his dad about what he had found out about his grandfather and that he may not have died as was thought for all of these years. The plane landed and he and Kevin immediately hailed a cab and headed directly to his childhood home. What he could not know was at that very moment Thomas Grant was boarding a plane bound for Maine with all of the answers that Jack was in search of.

Chapter 30

Bangor, Maine
January 2001

Thomas grimaced as he eased himself into the plane seat. The last direct flight to Bangor had departed hours ago, forcing him to route through Portland with a shuttle connection. He'd fall even further behind Jack's trail, but options were scarce. His ribs screamed with each breath–aftermath of the explosion that had nearly killed him. Proper recovery would require weeks of rest, a luxury he couldn't afford. Still, as the engines hummed to life, Thomas closed his eyes with unexpected relief. After days of constant movement, even this cramped airline seat felt like salvation.

The snow fell in thick, silent flakes that clung to Thomas's coat and melted against his feverish skin. It reminded him of that fateful night decades ago when he'd first approached Simon–another Douglas, another generation, another burden to place on innocent shoulders. Now he stood across the street, watching Jack and his father through the golden-lit study window, their silhouettes moving behind partially drawn curtains. The familiar weight of responsibility pressed down on Thomas's shoulders, heavier than the snow accumulating there. After all these years, the cycle was repeating itself in this small Maine town–the same crisp air that smelled of pine and woodsmoke, the same crunch of fresh powder beneath his boots, the same impossible choice to drag another of William Douglas's descendants into a war not of their making. Would this endless cycle ever break? Would he find peace before his final breath?

When Jack and Kevin arrived at the Douglas family home–a two-story colonial with warm light spilling from its windows against the darkening sky–Jack's mother flung open the heavy oak door. Her face, lined with worry, instantly transformed with relief.

"Oh thank God," she exclaimed, her voice breaking slightly as she pulled Jack into a fierce embrace that spoke of hours of anxiety. "Your father and I have been trying to reach you all day." She extended her arm to include Kevin in the hug, then quickly ushered them both inside, away from the biting cold and into the house that smelled of cinnamon and old books.

Jack dropped his bag by the doorway. "Why were you trying to reach us?"

His mother sank onto the sofa, worry lines creasing her forehead. "Your father's locked himself in his study since your call. He found something online he's desperate to show you."

"Dad's home?" Jack frowned. "I thought he'd be at work."

"Hasn't left that room all day." She shook her head, then noticed Kevin swaying slightly on his feet. "Oh, Kevin, you look exhausted."

Kevin collapsed onto the sofa cushions. "Finally, someone acknowledges my suffering."

"Let me get the guest room ready," she said, rising with motherly purpose. "Fresh sheets are just what you need."

"Bless you," Kevin mumbled, shooting Jack an accusatory glance. "Someone refused to let me sleep on the plane."

Jack's eyebrows shot up. "Dad's home!" He motioned to Kevin. "Let's go."

The study door creaked open to reveal his father hunched at the desk, bathed in the blue glow of his monitor. Dark circles shadowed George's eyes, his hair disheveled as if he'd been running his hands through it all night. He blinked twice before recognition dawned.

"Jack?" George rose unsteadily, gripping the edge of the desk. "I've been calling you for hours."

Before Jack could explain, his father sank back into his chair. "You need to see this." His voice carried an unfamiliar tremor.

"This?" Jack pulled the folded printout from his pocket and smoothed it on the desk.

George stared at the photograph, his mouth slightly open. A tear formed at the corner of his eye but didn't fall. The silence between them stretched taut with unspoken questions.

Jack placed a second image beside the first. "Kevin pulled this from D.C. police records. It's Thomas Grant–after the explosion."

Thomas stood motionless in the snow, his breath forming ghostly clouds that dissolved into the darkness. His cracked ribs throbbed beneath his coat as he weighed his options. Should he approach the warmly lit house directly, or wait in the bitter cold until Jack emerged alone? Exhaustion clouded his judgment. With Kevin and Jack's parents inside, the timing couldn't be worse–yet the urgency of his mission couldn't wait for perfect circumstances.

His feet made the decision before his mind could, carrying him across the street where his shoes left deep impressions in the virgin snow. The Douglas home loomed before him, windows glowing amber against the night. Each step up the salt-crusted porch stairs sent shooting pain through his torso. The brass doorbell felt ice-cold against his fingertip as he pressed it, hearing the muffled chime echo inside.

"Who could that be at this hour?" Jack's mother's voice carried through the door as she approached.

When the door swung open, Thomas stood framed in the entryway, snowflakes melting on his shoulders. He clutched his worn fedora in trembling fingers, the brim damp from precipitation. "Pardon the intrusion, ma'am. Is Mr. Jack Douglas available?" His voice was hoarse from the cold.

"Yes, he is." Her eyes narrowed slightly, taking in his disheveled appearance and the fading bruise near his temple.

"May I tell him who's calling?"

"Thomas," he replied with a polite nod, suppressing a wince as his ribs protested the movement.

Mrs. Douglas stepped back from the doorway, gesturing Thomas inside. "Please, come in from that awful cold. I'll fetch Jack for you."

Thomas shuffled across the threshold, his shoes leaving small puddles on the entryway rug.

"How about something hot to drink? Tea perhaps?" she offered.

"I appreciate the kindness, but no thank you." Thomas remained standing, hat still clutched in his hands. If his conversation with Jack went as expected, he doubted he'd be staying long enough to finish a cup.

"I'll just be a moment then." She disappeared down the hallway toward the study.

Jack looked up at the soft knock on the study door. His mother leaned in, her expression curious. "Jack, there's someone here to see you. A man named Thomas."

The name hung in the air like a thunderclap. Jack's eyes darted to Kevin, then to his father. The timing was impossible, they had just been discussing Thomas Grant, and now a Thomas was at their door?

"Did he mention why he's here?" Jack asked, his voice suddenly dry.

"No, he didn't say."

"Thanks, Mom. I'll be right out." As his mother's footsteps faded, Jack exchanged a loaded glance with Kevin.

"Dude," Kevin whispered, "what are the odds? Thomas? Right now?"

Jack rose from his father's leather chair, his movements deliberate. "Let's find out if coincidences really exist." Jack opened the door and froze. Standing in his parents' living room was the man from the photographs–flesh and blood instead of faded ink. Thomas Grant's weathered face bore the same deep-set eyes and prominent cheekbones, though now framed by silver-streaked hair and etched with decades of worry lines. Jack's mouth went dry. Thomas shifted uncomfortably under the scrutiny, his worn fedora clutched between calloused fingers, the brim damp and misshapen. The grandfather clock in the corner ticked away five, ten, fifteen seconds of stunned silence.

"I am Jack Douglas," Jack finally managed, his voice barely above a whisper. "Do I know you?"

"I am Thomas Grant," the man replied, his voice a gravelly baritone that carried the weight of years. "And no, we have never met."

"Yes, I know who you are." Jack's words hung in the air between them.

Thomas's eyes widened almost imperceptibly. He leaned slightly on his right leg, wincing as he redistributed his weight from what must have been an injury. His gaze darted briefly to the hallway behind Jack, then back to the young man's face.

"I'm sorry," Thomas said, each word carefully measured. "Did you say you know who I am?"

Chapter 31

Bangor, Maine
January 2001

Jack held up the old photograph of Thomas standing beside his grandfather Simon. "I've been expecting you."

Thomas staggered back, gripping the doorframe to steady himself. His mouth opened, but no words emerged.

"Holy shit!" Kevin burst into the room, eyes widening. "It really is him!"

Jack's mother appeared behind them, her brow furrowed. "Who exactly is this man that's causing such a commotion?"

"We have a lot to discuss, Mom." Jack never broke his gaze from Thomas's ashen face. "Perhaps you could bring some coffee to the study while our guest recovers from his surprise."

Jack gestured toward the study. "Mr. Grant, please join us in here."

Thomas hesitated in the doorway. "I'd prefer to speak with you privately," he said, his voice level despite the tension in his shoulders.

"That won't be necessary," Jack replied, crossing his arms. "Whatever you have to say concerns all of us."

Thomas surveyed the faces watching him–Jack's parents, Kevin hovering nearby–and realized he had little choice. Curiosity about what they already knew tugged at him as well.

"Very well," he conceded with a curt nod.

Jack turned to Kevin. "You should get some rest."

"Not a chance," Kevin said, stepping aside to let Thomas enter.

The night stretched long over coffee and cake as Thomas revealed everything, the ancient conflict between Protectors and Deceivers, the five gold watches with their immense power, the generations-long struggle. Throughout his account, Jack kept exchanging glances with his father, particularly during mentions of Simon. Thomas carefully sidestepped the truth about William Douglas, unwilling to reveal their extraterrestrial lineage with Kevin present. He concluded with his narrow escape from Beck in Washington just days earlier.

It was very late by the time Thomas finished his story. Jack and his father, George, had peppered him with questions throughout, and Thomas had answered each one without hesitation. The flood of inquiries peaked when Thomas revealed he was from another planet–and the last of the Protectors left on Earth.

“So if you’re the only Protector sent here, how do you expect to defeat the Deceivers, or even contain them? Eventually you’ll be gone, and nobody will know they ever existed. Then what?” Jack demanded.

“My directive forbids involving any humans in the struggle against the Deceivers,” Thomas replied, sidestepping the implication that he needed Jack’s help.

“Then why have you involved me in all this if you won’t involve humans?” George asked.

Thomas hesitated, fatigue from the earlier attack tugging at him. He glanced at Kevin, then back to George. “Maybe we should continue this conversation in private.”

“Kevin’s family,” Jack said firmly. “Anything you need to say, you can say to him.”

Thomas closed his eyes for a moment. “I don’t mean to be rude, but my directives are very clear on this matter.”

“My directive is clear too, Mr. Grant,” Jack countered. “So go on–answer my dad’s question.”

Thomas weighed his options. He’d come this far with Kevin in the room, and he doubted Jack would accept another refusal. “Very well. But you must understand–you may be putting your friend in grave danger.” He cast a quick look at Kevin.

“We understand,” Jack said without hesitation.

George cleared his throat. “Just a moment–maybe we should ask Kevin if he wants to stay for this.”

Jack turned to Kevin, who sat hunched in the leather armchair by the bay window, moonlight casting half his face in silver. "What do you say? Want to hear this even though it could put you in danger?"

Kevin's fingers drummed against the worn armrest. His eyes, bloodshot from the hours of revelations, darted between Jack and Thomas. "I'll stay if you want me here. Or step out if that's better." His voice cracked slightly, betraying the calm he was trying to project.

"You're family," Jack said firmly, the table lamp highlighting the determined set of his jaw. "I want you here."

Thomas leaned forward, his weathered hands clasped so tightly his knuckles whitened. "If this information reaches any Deceiver, the consequences would be catastrophic." His voice dropped to a near-whisper, forcing everyone to lean closer. "Before I continue, I need your solemn word that what I'm about to reveal never leaves this room." His piercing gaze moved from face to face, lingering on each pair of eyes.

Murmured promises filled the tense silence. Thomas drew a deep breath, his shoulders rising and falling beneath his worn tweed jacket. He fixed his gaze first on George's lined face, then on Jack's expectant one.

"The reason I sought you out, Jack, is that you, your father, and your grandfather are direct descendants of our leader." The words fell heavy as stones. "You and I are of the same people."

The grandfather clock in the corner ticked loudly in the silence that followed. Jack's face froze; his coffee cup suspended halfway to his lips. George's complexion paled to the color of the cream in his untouched dessert plate. Jack had mentally prepared for almost anything, had even pondered the photo caption about "good Aliens," but hearing the words spoken aloud transformed speculation into an undeniable reality that settled like a physical weight on his shoulders.

Chapter 32

Washington, D.C.
January 2001

The man who approached Susan had to duck slightly to clear the doorframe. His hand swallowed hers completely when he extended it in greeting.

"John Wells, head of security," he said with a voice that matched his frame. "What brings you to our hospital today, Detective?"

Susan had to tilt her head back to meet his gaze. The hospital badge clipped to his suit jacket hung at her eye level. She recognized him immediately–Wells had been a defensive tackle for the Redskins until a career-ending knee injury five years ago. Now he patrolled hospital corridors instead of offensive lines, though his six-foot-eight, three-hundred-pound frame still commanded the same respect.

Susan shook his massive hand. "I hope I'm not interrupting anything important, Mr. Wells."

"Just wrestling with paperwork." Wells shifted his weight, making the floor creak beneath him. "Never-ending battle."

Susan's neck strained as she looked up at him. "I need to check your security footage. We're tracking someone who reportedly visited this morning."

"Shouldn't be a problem." Wells gestured for her to follow. "We can review the tapes in my office." His "office" turned out to be little more than a converted storage closet–a cramped box with a desk buried under paperwork and several monitors mounted on one wall.

Wells pointed to a battered leather chair; its cushion patched with strips of duct tape. "Have a seat. Which floor am I looking for?"

"Fourth floor," Susan said, hoping the grainy footage would reveal what she needed. Wells paused at the doorway. "I'll grab the tape. Need anything to drink while you wait?"

"I'm fine, thanks," Susan said.

Alone in the cramped office, Susan studied the wall of photos opposite the monitors. Wells stood beaming beside his family in one frame, arm-in-arm with celebrities in others. The former NFL defensive tackle's massive frame looked almost comical next to the tiny desk. From stadium roars to security monitors–quite the career change.

Wells returned, brandishing a VHS tape. "Got it."

"Can we start around nine this morning?" Susan asked, pulling her chair closer as he loaded the tape.

"Sure thing." He handed her a remote. "Basic controls–just like your VCR at home."

His radio crackled. Wells sighed, unclipping it from his belt. "Duty calls. ER never sleeps." He headed for the door. "Take your time. Door locks automatically when you leave."

Susan sat in the small office with remote in hand and scanned the video from earlier in the day. There has got to be a better way to do this, it could take forever to find anything on these tapes, Susan thought to herself. After about ten minutes of searching, she found what she was looking for, the police Commissioner and another man at the nurse's station on the fourth floor. She didn't recognize the man with the Commissioner, but her instincts told her that he wasn't with the D.C. Police, and if he wasn't with the Police then what was he doing there and why would the Commissioner bring a civilian along on police business? There wasn't much more to view on the tapes, she watched until the Commissioner and the other man turned and left.

Susan left a hastily scribbled thank-you note on Wells's desk. Her cell phone vibrated against her hip just as she reached for the doorknob.

"Detective Young," she answered, pressing the phone to her ear.

Commissioner Black's voice crackled through the speaker. He wanted a briefing on the Grant case–immediately.

"I'll be there in ten minutes, sir," she promised, though her mind raced with questions. The Commissioner personally requesting updates on a case with a missing victim and almost no leads? Something didn't add up.

The five-mile drive to headquarters stretched into a thirty-minute crawl through midday traffic. Susan drummed her fingers against the steering wheel, rehearsing what little information she had. When she finally reached the front desk, the officer there lifted a red phone receiver and announced her arrival, his eyes never leaving his computer screen.

The officer hung up the phone. "Go right up, he is expecting you," he said, jabbing a finger toward the bank of elevators with their polished brass doors gleaming under the fluorescent lights.

Susan had only been to the main headquarters once before–the day she'd filled out her hiring paperwork in triplicate, before being exiled to the cramped precinct west of the Capitol. The elevator ascended with a silky hum that made her precinct's grinding lift seem like ancient machinery. When the doors parted on the eighth floor, the scent of lemon polish and expensive cologne washed over her.

She stepped onto carpet thick enough to swallow footsteps and entered a sitting area that stretched before her like a museum exhibit of power. At the far side, behind a mahogany desk that reflected the recessed lighting, sat an officer–a woman with immaculate posture and not a single wrinkle in her uniform. The walls gleamed with dark walnut paneling that probably cost more than Susan's annual salary, while butter-soft leather furniture–arranged with mathematical precision–looked pristine, as if for display only. Susan's mind flashed to her own workspace: a scarred desk wedged into a cubicle where she could touch both walls if she stretched her arms.

"Detective Young?" the woman asked, her voice as crisp as her appearance as Susan approached.

Susan nodded. "Detective Young for Commissioner Black."

The receptionist, who couldn't have been more than twenty-five, rose from her chair and gestured toward a hallway. "This way, please." Her polished shoes made no sound on the plush carpet as she led Susan to an imposing set of double doors. She rapped twice, then opened one door just wide enough to lean in. "Detective Young to see you, sir." The officer held the door open with a practiced gesture. "Commissioner will see you now, Detective."

Susan stepped into a space that could have housed her entire precinct's detective division. Dark walnut paneling climbed the walls toward a coffered ceiling, framing a desk that dominated the center of the room like a judge's bench. Her gaze drifted to a museum-quality display case stretching along the far wall. Behind glass that caught no fingerprints rested artifacts of power and violence–a pristine confederate Civil War officer's uniform, a Thompson submachine gun mounted on velvet, and other historical treasures arranged with curatorial precision.

The quarterly budget memo denying her precinct's request for updated computers flashed through her mind as her shoes sank into carpet thick enough to muffle artillery fire.

“Detective, thank you for stopping in, please take a seat,” Commissioner Black said as he pointed to a large leather chair.

“I know you must be busy so I will do my best to keep this short,” Commissioner Black said as he sat down behind his desk. “What can you tell me about, Mr. Grant, the man who was nearly killed the other night?” Black said as he set his gaze on Susan.

“Not too much on him sir, he doesn't appear to have any family that I was able to locate; he seemed to be in the wrong place at the wrong time,” Susan said not planning to share any more than she had too.

“You spoke with him this morning; did he say where he was going?” Black asked his dark eyes fixed on Susan.

Susan shook her head. "No, I had absolutely no idea he'd bolt from the hospital. The man could barely talk let alone get out of bed and walk away when I interviewed him."

The Commissioner's pen hammered against his notebook like a metronome counting down her career. His eyes never left her face–cold, predatory, dissecting.

"What made him so desperate to flee?" Black's pen stopped mid-tap. The sudden silence felt more threatening than the noise.

"I can only speculate." Susan leaned forward. "Maybe he feared those thugs would return to finish what they started." She studied Black's face for any reaction; any tell that might explain his obsession with this case.

"So you have nothing." Black's voice dripped with contempt. "Absolutely nothing on this man, and zero explanation for why he'd rip out his IVs and vanish."

Susan's face burned as blood rushed to her cheeks. Her jaw clenched so tight she could hear her teeth grinding. This wasn't embarrassment–this was pure, white-hot rage at his tone and his continued refusal to explain his interest.

"With all due respect, sir, the man was a victim. He committed no crime by nearly dying." Each word came out clipped, precise.

"I will be the one who determines when this investigation ends," Black hissed, slamming his palm against the desk.

"Yes sir." Susan's fingernails dug crescents into her palms beneath the desk.

“What can you tell me about the gold pocket watch that was found on him?” Black asked his tone a bit softer. “Nothing, I didn’t look at it,” Susan said even more confused by the last question. “Didn’t you give him his personal belongings back when you went back to the hospital to speak with him?” Black asked, his stare still burning into Susan.

“Yes, I did give him his belongings, but I did not look at the items in the bag myself,” Susan answered.

Susan began really questioning what was going on, the Commissioner was not asking her any questions he couldn’t read for himself in her report that had been already filed. It appeared to her that he didn’t want her to know why he was so interested in this particular case.

“I see,” Black said, “Is there any more you would like to add about the case?” the Commissioner asked as he sat down his pen.

Susan thought to herself for a moment, Black still hadn’t given her any idea what this was all about, so she thought she would throw some bait out in the water and see if she would get a nibble.

“No, nothing really, I am about to put the finishing touches on this one, all I plan to do is run over to the hospital again and get with their security department,” Susan said thinking to herself if there was anything going on this would let her know that her hunch that Black’s interest in this case had nothing to do with the police.

“Their Security Department? What do you need to see them about?” Black asked the question Susan had hoped he would.

“It’s probably nothing sir, but when I went back to speak with Mr. Grant today one of the nurses who had been on duty said that two men had been there looking for Mr. Grant, but he had already checked out,” Susan said as she paid close attention to Commissioner Black’s reaction to this information.

Black didn’t show any change in his face or his tone when she asked, “Did the nurse happen to say who the two men were or what they looked like?”

“No, she couldn’t remember but suggested that I check with security because everything is monitored on video and I would be able to get a look at who the men were from the tapes,” Susan said waiting for the bait to be taken.

“Do you think that there is anything to this?” Black asked as casually as before.

“I doubt it, but since he told me he didn’t know anyone in town and has no family that I can find, who would even know he was there, unless it was the men who had almost killed him.” Susan said as she began to think that Black was not going to take the bait and that perhaps her gut feeling about him hiding something was wrong.

“I think we’re done here Detective, I want to thank you for your time today,” Black said as he stood up from his desk. “I think you’re right, this case has run its course, in fact let me save you the time, I will have my assistant call over and speak with the hospital about the tape and if anything turns up I will give you a call,” Commissioner Black said as he came around the desk to shake Susan’s hand and walk her to the door.

“It’s really no trouble,” Susan said, I drive by there on my way home,” Susan said as she smiled inside knowing that the Commissioner had just taken the bait and confirmed her feeling that he knew more about this situation than he was letting on.

“I insist, it is the least I can do after taking up so much of your time today and besides these hospitals can be difficult in releasing that sort of stuff without a fight, I think throwing the weight of my office behind the request should shake things up and get results,” Black said as they reached the door.

“Thank you, Commissioner, I guess that couldn’t hurt,” Susan said trying not to laugh at his attempt to pretend to help and not knowing she knew he was just trying to cover his tracks.

Why he was trying to cover his tracks she didn’t know, but one thing she did know was this case was far from over, just one quick phone call and then off to do some digging into the past of one Mr. Black.

Chapter 33

Ulm Germany
December 1942

It took a moment for Simon to gather himself after the sudden commotion, he looked at one of the guards slumped against the wall and then turned and saw Thomas standing a few steps away.

"What happened?" Simon asked as he looked around at both of the SS guards lying incapacitated in the tavern.

"Herr Walker came and told me you were in trouble, I couldn't let them take you," Thomas said very casually as he motioned to Herr Walker standing behind that bar with a startled look on his face.

"What was that flash I saw?" Simon asked.

"It was my black case, there are some built in protections that I can call upon when needed," Thomas answered knowing that there was no reason to try and deceive anyone about what they had seen.

"Are they dead?" Simon asked as he looked again at the guards lying on the floor.

"Yes," Thomas answered quietly.

It took a few minutes for the men to hide the bodies of the dead SS guards and make plans for what they were going to do next. It was obvious that Beck had found out that Simon was an imposter and it was only a matter of time before more SS guards showed up looking for them; getting out of Germany alive was not looking good at the moment.

Simon waited as Thomas talked with Herr Walker and his brother, he could not make out what was being said but he was very sure that they had seen more than Thomas would have liked and some sort of explanation was in order.

After a few moments the conversation broke up and Thomas turned to Simon, "Come, we do not have much time before the guards are missed and more come in search of them."

Thomas and Simon were led into the same room that Herr Walker had taken Thomas to hide.

“What are we going to do now?” Simon asked worried about their current situation.

“We are in grave danger; I should have never risked bringing you here,” Thomas said as he sat on the edge of the small cot.

“I realize we are in grave danger, remember I was the one who was nearly shot by those two goons,” Simon said as he paced the floor of the small room. “How long can we stay in here before they find us?” Simon added.

“We are going to wait until dark and then try and make our escape.” Thomas answered.

“Escape? How are we going to do that? This whole town will be crawling with soldiers looking for us,” Simon said in a bit of a panic. “How did Beck find out about us?”

Thomas took a piece of paper from his pocket and handed it to Simon.

“What is this? I can’t read it.” Simon said as he looked at the paper and the strange writing on it.

“That is how Beck knows you are not who you claim to be,” Thomas said frustrated with himself that he didn’t realize this sooner.

“What does it say?” Simon asked, trying to understand how Beck could even know. Thomas explained that the paper contained names of other Deceivers in the German government and on the list are four very high-ranking members of the Government and numerous generals and political figures. Beck, as the lead scientist and one of the leaders of the Deceivers, is in constant communication with the other Deceivers and that is how he had been able to determine Simon had not been sent by anyone from Berlin.

After hiding for over an hour, Thomas and Simon tensed at the soft rap against the door. Herr Walker's hushed voice filtered through: "It is dark now. You must leave before they return." Simon gripped Thomas's arm. "The weapon–if we flee now, the Nazis will deploy it against our forces. Everything we've risked will be for nothing."

Thomas slumped against the damp stone wall, his face ashen in the dim light of the single bulb swinging overhead. "There is nothing we can do," he whispered, fingers trembling as they gripped his black case. "Now that Beck knows who we are, there is no way we can get close to the machine." His eyes, normally so determined, now reflected only defeat as he stared at the cracked floorboards beneath his polished shoes.

Simon paced the cramped room, the wooden boards creaking beneath his weight. Sweat beaded on his forehead despite the cellar's chill. "If we can get inside the main building–there are no guards there, just Beck and his assistant working on the machine." He stopped abruptly, turning to face Thomas. "You've done it once already, through that underground tunnel before you came to Maine. Why can't we do it again?"

Thomas's weathered face remained motionless for a long moment, the silence broken only by distant shouts of SS guards. Finally, he sighed, his breath visible in the cold air. "Yes, that is true," he conceded, running a hand through his silver-streaked hair. "But at that time, I moved about without worry. Now..." His voice trailed off as his gaze drifted to the door, beyond which lay danger. "Now we'll be captured the moment we're spotted. Or worse–shot on sight."

"We must try," Simon insisted, his eyes blazing with intensity. There is too much at risk to simply do nothing."

Thomas rubbed his temples. "Getting inside is only half the battle. Without knowing where Beck keeps the watch, our mission is futile. Even if we destroy this weapon, they'll simply build another."

"The watch never leaves Beck's person," Simon replied with quiet certainty, though his confidence stemmed more from instinct than evidence.

Thomas hesitated, weighing the impossible odds against the catastrophic consequences of inaction. Outside their hidden sanctuary, boots pounded on cobblestones as SS troops stormed through Ulm, ransacking homes and businesses. The weapon facility stood empty, its construction halted while Beck and his assistant Gray led the manhunt that had transformed the peaceful Bavarian town into an armed camp.

Beck stormed into the tavern, his polished boots gleaming under the dim lights as he interrogated Herr Walker and his brother with cold precision. His eyes, gray as winter steel, narrowed with each response. The SS weren't just hunting Simon and Thomas–they were combing every inch of Ulm for their two missing comrades, whose bodies lay hidden beneath the tavern's ancient wine barrels. From their cramped hiding place, Simon and Thomas could hear the methodical thud of jackboots in the corridor, each footfall sending dust motes dancing in the thin shaft of light beneath the door.

Simon's shirt clung to his back with cold sweat as he pressed himself against the rough stone wall, not daring to breathe when a shadow paused outside. Thomas had meticulously coached Herr Walker on his story–that the fugitives had fled north toward Stuttgart after receiving his warning.

At midnight, the door's rusted hinges protested softly as Herr Walker slipped inside, his weathered face ghostly in the feeble candlelight. "The guards have moved to the eastern quarter, and Beck has retreated to his villa on the hill," he whispered, his breath visible in the cellar's damp chill. Thomas's fingers tightened around his black case, knuckles whitening.

"The time is now." His voice was barely audible as he clasped Herr Walker's calloused hand in gratitude. With a final nod, they emerged from their sanctuary, creeping down the corridor where ancient floorboards threatened to announce their presence with every step. Ahead lay the tavern's rear exit and beyond that, the moonlit streets of Ulm–a gauntlet they must run with death as the only prize for failure.

Chapter 34

Bangor, Maine
January 2001

The soft crunch of snow under Jack and Thomas' shoes was the only sound on the crisp Maine morning; the two had been walking for five minutes or so without a word being spoken. Jack was lost in thought about everything that Thomas had revealed; it was tough to grasp everything all at once. Thomas understood that it must be tough for Jack and his family and though he felt like he had divulged too much to Jack's parents and to Kevin, he felt it had to be done. He had not slept since he left the hospital and was feeling very tired, but he didn't want to refuse Jack's invitation to take a walk with him.

They rounded a small stand of trees that opened to a field, at the edge of the field was an old stone building. Thomas knew what it was as soon as it came into view, it was the old mill where he had told Simon on that night in 1942 the same thing he had just told Jack and his family. Thomas had come here often during the years since his good friend disappeared that night in Ulm Germany.

The plan had been for them to meet here once their mission had been completed, but in the chaos that ensued on the night they took the watch and the weapon from the Nazis, Simon had saved his life only to fall victim to the weapon that Beck had been developing. It was a memory that still was fresh in Thomas' mind as if it had just happened last week instead of nearly sixty years ago.

Jack was the first to speak, "I used to come here when I was small, I thought that I would find some clue or something about what had happened to my grandfather and we would be able to find him," Jack said as he looked at the old building off in the distance.

"I return here often as well Thomas said," as he told Jack of his agreement to meet Simon at the mill once they escaped Germany and the Deceivers.

Jack's voice broke the silence. "My father visits this place too, though he thinks I don't know. I've watched him from the mill loft and from between the trees, just standing there for hours."

They trudged onward through the snow, their footprints marking a path toward the weathered structure.

"Have you reached a decision?" Thomas finally asked.

Jack kept his eyes forward. "There's only one choice I can make. I'll help you stop the Deceivers and recover those watches."

Thomas nodded, relief washing over him. Jack was fulfilling his destiny–the natural leader Thomas had always believed him to be. But before he could fully appreciate this victory, Jack stopped abruptly.

"But I have conditions," Jack said, turning to face him. "My father and Kevin join us. That's non-negotiable."

Thomas's relief evaporated. "That's impossible. I cannot permit it."

"You don't have much choice. Your solo mission hasn't exactly been a success story."

"The fewer people involved, the better," Thomas countered. "My instructions explicitly forbid dragging humans into our conflict."

Jack's eyes narrowed. "And how's your solo mission been working out?" He gestured at the snow-covered landscape. "My father has Protector blood, and Kevin already knows everything. That's my offer–non-negotiable."

Without waiting for an answer, Jack turned and trudged back toward his parents' house, boots crunching through the fresh powder.

Thomas remained motionless, weighing his limited options. He couldn't undo what Jack's father and Kevin now knew. And if he was honest with himself, his solitary efforts had barely kept the Deceivers contained–at tremendous personal cost.

"Very well," Thomas said, hurrying to catch up. "Perhaps additional allies would help. But they must understand the Deceivers will hunt them relentlessly once their involvement is discovered."

Jack clapped him on the shoulder, his expression lightening. "That's why you've got me. Now let's grab breakfast and get some rest. We'll strategize later."

Chapter 35

Washington, D.C.
January 2001

Back in her apartment after the meeting with Commissioner Black, Susan stood at her kitchen counter, absently stirring a pot of soup she wasn't hungry for. The Grant case should have been straightforward–wrong place, wrong time–but Black's unusual interest nagged at her. His questions had been too pointed, his demeanor too controlled.

She abandoned the soup, grabbed a cold slice of pizza from the fridge and popped open a Diet Pepsi instead. At her computer, she typed Black's name into various databases, trying every search trick she knew. An hour later, her screen reflected nothing but dead ends–eerily similar to when she'd searched for Thomas Grant. The digital void where a person's history should exist felt deliberate, manufactured. The only thread connecting Black to anything was his relationship with Senator Buckley from California. A single newspaper article mentioned Buckley had personally recommended Black for Commissioner, accompanied by a photo of the Senator mid-speech, hand raised dramatically to emphasize some forgotten point.

Susan powered down her computer and stared into the darkened screen. Commissioner Black was a ghost–no digital footprint, no history. The wall clock read 11:05 PM. Late, but not too late. She tugged on her worn Snoopy and gang sweatshirt, snatched her car keys from the counter, and headed for the precinct. The police database might reveal what civilian resources couldn't.

Rain had replaced the earlier snowfall, pattering against her windshield as she navigated empty streets. Within minutes, she pulled into her reserved spot and dashed through the downpour to the station entrance. Inside, only the night desk sergeant and a couple of officers populated the fluorescent-lit space. Perfect. The fewer witnesses to her after-hours investigation into her boss, the better.

Susan stared at the screen, the cursor blinking mockingly at her. Ten minutes of searching had yielded nothing–not a single record of Black's existence before his appointment. She gnawed on her pencil, the wood splintering slightly between her teeth. Every commissioner she'd ever known had climbed the ranks, leaving paper trails, commendations, and at least a few enemies. Black had none of these.

On impulse, she dialed the National Mall Security Office, wincing when she noticed the time on her desk clock.

"Security Operations, Officer Daniels speaking."

"Detective Susan Young, D.C. Metro." She straightened in her chair. "I need access to surveillance footage from the attack on Thomas Grant outside the Natural History Museum last week."

"One moment, Detective."

As Daniels's hold music droned in her ear, Susan drummed her fingers on the desk. Even if the footage showed the attackers clearly, connecting them to Black was a long shot. Still, her instincts were screaming.

"Detective? Those tapes were requisitioned today. Senator Buckley's office. National security matter."

Susan's hand tightened around the receiver. "Buckley. Of course it was. Did his people pick them up personally?"

"Let me check... the log just shows the requisition form, signed by someone from his office. Says 'National Security' and not much else." "Thank you, Officer Daniels. You've been very helpful." Susan hung up, a chill running through her that had nothing to do with the precinct's ancient heating system. The pieces were aligning too perfectly to be coincidence.

Susan leaned back in her chair, the vinyl creaking beneath her weight. The threads were unraveling faster than she could follow them. Confronting a U.S. Senator about attempted murder wasn't exactly in her job description.

She massaged her temples. Why would Black and Buckley want Grant dead? What secret was worth killing for? Whatever Grant was mixed up in, it was big enough to involve people who could erase their own histories.

Hours later, Susan stared at her bedroom ceiling, sleep a distant possibility. The case had burrowed under her skin. Academy instructors had drilled it into them: when a simple case hits nothing but walls, you're dealing with something engineered to appear simple. The complete absence of background on Black wasn't just unusual–it was impossible without significant resources and influence.

As dawn approached, Susan was already in her kitchen, mechanically stirring instant coffee while the morning news droned. Senator Buckley appeared on screen, gesturing emphatically before some manufacturing plant. Susan froze mid-stir. Behind him stood a familiar figure–the same man she'd glimpsed with Black at the hospital. Her spoon clattered against the counter as she approached the screen.

"You," she whispered, tapping the man's pixelated face. "You're my missing piece."

Chapter 36

Washington, D.C.
January 2001

Beck leaned forward in his chair across from Commissioner Black's desk, both men focused on the problem of Detective Susan Young.

"After questioning her extensively, I'm confident she has no knowledge of our operation," Commissioner Black said, his voice carrying clearly through the speaker phone. "Excellent news," came Senator Buckley's voice from the device. "With the watch in our possession, we can proceed with constructing the new machine." "And what of Grant?" Beck inquired, his brow furrowing. "He still has the other watch. "Senator Buckley's tone turned calculating. "Perhaps we can use this detective to our advantage. Give her a special assignment tracking down our elusive Mr. Grant. Let her do the legwork for us."

A slow, calculating smile spread across Commissioner Black's face, mirrored by Beck across the desk.

"Brilliant strategy Senator," Black said, tapping his fingers together. "I'll monitor her every move while she unwittingly leads us straight to the watch."

"I've arranged NSA clearance for the new facility," Senator Buckley's voice crackled through the speaker. "Beck, you and Gray will commence construction immediately. The project reports directly to my office alone." His tone hardened. "Gentlemen, we're too close to tolerate any missteps now."

Black straightened his tie. "Detective Young will be assigned to our special project by morning. She'll be thoroughly distracted."

"Perfect." Senator Buckley's laugh crackled through the speaker. "Though I doubt she'll uncover anything useful. Most of your detectives couldn't find a lighthouse in a storm. Still, when Grant inevitably surfaces, we'll have our second watch."

The call continued as they cemented the details: construction timelines for the machine, security protocols, and the final phases of their global domination strategy. Beck checked his watch–not the golden one concealed in his breast pocket, but his ordinary Rolex. In six hours, they would convene at the secure facility to activate their prize and unlock its secrets.

All three men stood in a small outer office with peeling beige paint and water-stained ceiling tiles, located precisely five blocks northeast of the Pentagon. The nondescript, four-story, concrete building blended seamlessly with its bureaucratic neighbors, its windows coated with years of city grime. Once bustling with classified military communications during the Cold War, it had sat abandoned for a decade, its existence nearly forgotten in government property records. Senator Buckley had personally selected this location, smirking as he signed requisition forms that diverted NSA black budget funds to renovate what was listed as "Strategic Communications Facility 47-B." The Senator's jowly face now gleamed with satisfaction in the harsh fluorescent light–right under Washington's nose, hidden by classification protocols he himself had helped design, the Deceivers would operate with impunity.

"Let us open the watch," Senator Buckley commanded, lowering his substantial frame into a squeaking government-issue chair behind a battered gray metal desk.

Beck's fingers trembled slightly as he extracted the gleaming gold timepiece from his breast pocket. The watch's polished surface caught the light as he placed it reverently on the desk's scratched surface. His mouth went dry; after decades of searching, after losing their previous watch to Thomas Grant and his mysterious ally–a man whose identity had frustrated their global intelligence network for years–they finally had another of the five legendary devices in their possession.

In the smoke-filled aftermath of Berlin's bombing raids, as their prized machine and watch slipped through bloodied fingers, Buckley and Beck had marshaled the full might of their shadow network. They dispatched dead-eyed operatives to comb through the rubble of European capitals, infiltrated Allied intelligence services, and emptied Swiss bank accounts funding their desperate quest. Gray and Black orchestrated interrogations in dank basement rooms across three continents, extracting whispers about the five golden timepieces that gleamed with unearthly perfection. Despite intercepting cryptic communications about two watches in North America, their efforts crumbled alongside Hitler's Reich. As Soviet tanks rolled through Brandenburg Gate, the Deceivers slipped away on a moonless night, carrying briefcases of blueprints that would buy them sanctuary in Stalin's empire–leaving behind only corpses and questions about the scattered watches that held the universe's secrets.

The golden watch gleamed under the buzzing fluorescent lights as it sat on the desk's scratched metal surface. Beck's manicured fingers trembled slightly as he reached down and pressed the crown. The watch face split open with a barely audible click, and a shimmering holographic projection erupted from within–bathing their stunned faces in pulsing blue light. Equations, diagrams, and strange symbols hovered in the air, rotating slowly as if suspended in invisible liquid.

"This isn't weapon schematics," Beck whispered, his throat suddenly dry. The watch they had possessed in Ulm before the Allied bombing had contained blueprints for devastating energy weapons and the key to zero-point energy. But this–this was something else entirely. The projection showed what appeared to be a tear in the fabric of reality itself, with mathematical formulas spiraling around it. "Time travel," Senator Buckley breathed, his jowls quivering with excitement as he leaned forward, eyes reflecting the dancing blue light. "Not just theories–complete engineering specifications."

Commissioner Black's thin lips curved into a predatory smile as he circled the desk, his shadow cutting through the projection. "We assumed all five watches contained identical information," he said, watching as page after page of impossible science materialized before them. "Each must contain different pieces of the Protectors' technology." The three Deceivers exchanged glances across the hologram, their centuries-old dream of planetary domination suddenly expanding beyond even their ambitious imaginations.

Chapter 37

Ulm, Germany
December 1942

Thomas and Simon left the safety of the hidden room, the damp stone walls giving way to the crisp night air as they made their way back toward the Inn. The cobblestone streets, normally bustling with life, now lay eerily silent under the watchful eyes of SS guards whose numbers had doubled since their escape. German shepherds strained against leather leashes, their hot breath visible in the frigid air as they sniffed frantically for human scent. Orders to shoot on sight had been issued to all guards, their gloved fingers resting nervously on triggers of polished Luger pistols.

Against Beck's better judgment, he had put the hawk-faced Herr Fredrick in charge–Beck's obsession with the machine had grown too strong, his pale eyes bloodshot from sleepless nights as he neared completion of his work.

Herr Walker, a stooped man with calloused hands and a perpetual tremor, had revealed to Thomas and Simon a secret tunnel–its entrance concealed behind a rusted coal chute–that would take them to the edge of town near an abandoned farmhouse. From there, they would need to navigate the moonlit fields back to the imposing red brick building where the machine hummed with otherworldly energy.

Thomas's weathered face creased with concern; this route meant too much time exposed in open terrain, but their options had dwindled to nothing. After trudging several hundred yards through the tunnel, their boots splashing through puddles of stagnant water, they reached a set of rotting wooden stairs. The ancient wood creaked beneath their weight as they climbed toward a small door that opened into the pitch-black cellar. Herr Walker had assured them, his voice barely above a whisper, that the house had been abandoned for years, its previous occupants long since disappeared in the night. The SS would have already searched it once and moved on.

Thomas eased the door open, wincing at each groan of rusted hinges, and they entered the cellar. The musty air, thick with the scent of decay and rodent droppings, filled their lungs as they stood motionless, straining to hear any movement from above. Thomas gripped the silver weapon, its cool metal surface pulsing faintly with alien technology, ready to defend them should the need arise again.

After a few moments of standing in complete silence Thomas took from his inner pocket the small black case and it suddenly started to glow and light the room around them. Thomas moved the black case around to get a better look at the cellar and to try and locate a way out. Across the room in the corner the light showed a small set of stairs leading out of the cellar, Thomas and Simon made their way to the stairs and began to quietly make their way up. At the top of the stairs was an old wooden door that had nearly rotted off its hinges, again they paused at the door to listen for any sound of the searching guards.

When no sound was heard Thomas turned the light off and moved to open the door, when the door crashed to the floor. The sound was so loud that Thomas and Simon felt sure that anyone within a mile of the old house would surely have heard the commotion.

They waited in the main floor of the house, Thomas on one side looking out what once was a window and Simon was at the rear of the house looking through one of the bedroom windows that was still in place. The two of them waited for any sign that someone nearby had heard the door fall to the floor.

After what seemed like an hour Simon heard Thomas whisper for him to return to the front of the house. There was no moon that night as clouds had moved back in and made for better cover as they made their way out of the house and into the cold dark night of Ulm Germany.

Shadows became their allies as they crept through the night. Only the betraying crunch of frozen snow beneath their boots threatened to announce their presence. For half an hour they skirted the town's edge, making their way toward the imposing red brick structure. In the distance, several SS guards retreated toward the town square, but their path remained mercifully clear. Thomas guided them to a weathered woodshed adjacent to a smaller brick outbuilding that jutted from the main facility housing Beck and his machine.

"Through there," Thomas breathed, indicating the small structure with a subtle nod. "That tunnel leads directly to where they're keeping it."

Simon eyed the guard shelter mere yards from their destination. "And what about him?" he whispered. "How do we get past without being spotted?"

Thomas withdrew the small black case from his pocket. "I'll create a diversion to draw the guard away," he whispered, his finger tracing the device's surface. "Fortunate for us they've concentrated their forces in the city."

Simon eyed the lone sentry, who stood rigid with his rifle at the ready. "He looks trigger-happy enough to shoot at shadows," he muttered, recognizing the same guard who'd been posted when Thomas had first infiltrated the facility.

"That's precisely who we need to distract," Thomas replied, raising the case. "When I say run, don't hesitate."

A brilliant sphere of light erupted from the device, arcing through the darkness before plunging into the snow beyond the guard post.

"Now!" Thomas hissed, launching forward.

Simon bolted across the open ground, his heart hammering as his boots barely skimmed the snow's surface. Behind him, the guard abandoned his post, drawn to the mysterious glow like a moth to flame.

Reaching the door first, Simon's hands met cold metal. "It's chained shut," he called as Thomas arrived, breathless. "Impossible," Thomas gasped, glancing back at the guard who was still examining the melted crater. "They've upgraded security since my last visit."

His fingers worked frantically over the black case as he pressed it against the lock. The chain suddenly slackened and fell with a muffled thud into the snow.

"Inside, quickly," Thomas urged.

The guard lingered at the crater in the snow, baffled by the perfect circular depression where the light had vanished. He knelt, removed his glove, and felt the rim–still warm despite the freezing air. After a final glance at the inexplicable phenomenon, he straightened his shoulders and trudged back to his post, rifle clutched tightly against his chest.

Meanwhile, Thomas and Simon navigated the narrow tunnel, their breath forming ghostly clouds in the damp air. As the dim glow from the main facility became visible ahead, they pressed their backs against the cold stone wall and exchanged a tense nod. The moment of reckoning had arrived.

Simon's pulse quickened as he met Thomas's gaze. Failure meant death–not just theirs, but countless others if the Deceivers' machine launched. Yet retreat wasn't an option now.

Thomas slipped through the doorway into the main room, pressing himself against the wall to remain invisible. From his position at the threshold, Simon watched, waiting for the signal. Crouched low, Thomas navigated along the water main, gradually ascending to the building's upper level. Once in position, he flashed two fingers–their agreed sign.

Simon began his approach toward the machine, its metallic surface gleaming under the dim lights. The facility seemed deserted, no sign of Beck anywhere. Then, without warning, a small hatch on the craft slid open.

Thomas froze; his breath caught in his throat. Simon had disappeared to the far side of the machine, completely unaware that Beck had just emerged from the craft. The distance between Thomas and Beck was too great for an effective shot. He needed another plan–fast.

While Simon crept along the craft's hull, intent on planting the explosive device inside, Beck paused at the building's exit. He was moments from alerting Gray about the machine's readiness when something caught his peripheral vision. As Beck pivoted toward the movement, a brilliant flash of light struck him squarely in the chest, launching him backward into a wooden table with a splintering crash.

The commotion startled Simon, who hesitated in the shadows, uncertain whether to retreat or investigate. Then came Thomas's urgent whisper. Following the sound, Simon rounded the craft to find Thomas standing over Beck's unconscious form amid the wreckage of the table.

"What happened?" Simon whispered, rushing forward.

Thomas knelt, rifling through Beck's pockets. "He came out of the craft. I wasn't sure you'd spotted him."

Simon knelt beside Beck's motionless form. "Did you kill him?"

"No," Thomas said, rifling through Beck's pockets. "The blast was too weak at this distance." His fingers closed around something solid. "Plant the bomb in the craft. Quickly."

Thomas extracted a gold pocket watch, its chain ending in a distinctive silver ring. His eyes narrowed with recognition. This particular watch–the one containing secrets of energy and flight–had been Beck's blueprint for the craft and other Nazi weapons designed to crush the

Allies.

With practiced movements, Thomas adjusted the watch's knob before pocketing it. "Your watch," Thomas demanded, extending his palm.

Simon handed it over. Thomas made identical adjustments before returning it.

"It's a weapon now," Thomas explained. "Point the face and press the knob to fire." Simon stared at the watch with newfound wariness. "You might have mentioned that earlier."

"And risk you shooting me by accident?" Thomas grunted as he dragged Beck toward a steel pole. "Now hurry. We need that bomb placed before we're discovered."

Simon quickly went into the craft with the bomb. It was amazing; the technology used to develop this craft was truly from another world. Simon remembered Beck telling him that the craft was indestructible from the outside and the only way to destroy the craft would be from the inside at its power source. Once inside the craft Simon was truly amazed, the craft had no engine like an airplane or car. It seemed to work on some sort of invisible power that appeared to counteract gravity and what was most amazing was it made no sound and did not appear to need fuel. While Simon was inside the craft, Thomas was out in the main room, he had just finished tying Beck to a steel pole and was waiting for Simon to exit the craft so they could escape back through the tunnel before the craft and possibly the entire building was destroyed.

The door across the main room swung open. Gray stepped through, intending to update Beck on the search. Instead, he froze at the sight of Beck bound to the steel pole and a stranger standing nearby with his back turned. In one fluid motion, Gray drew his weapon and charged. Thomas heard the approaching footsteps and spun around, barely diving clear as a beam of energy sizzled past him. He crashed into the splintered remains of the table and tumbled to the floor. As he scrambled for his fallen silver weapon, Gray closed the distance between them.

From inside the craft, Simon heard the commotion. He rushed to the doorway and saw Gray looming over Thomas, aiming a device identical to Thomas's own. Gray's finger tensed on the trigger. Without conscious thought, Simon found himself drawing the watch from his pocket and leveling it at Gray.

"Freeze!" Simon called out, his voice steadier than his hands. "One move and I'll fire," he added, hoping the watch would actually work as Thomas had claimed. Gray spun around quickly and in the same motion fired his weapon at Simon.

The blast glanced off the side of the craft just inches from Simon. When Gray turned Thomas took his chance to act, he jumped up from the floor and landed on the back of Gray and wrestled him to the ground. The two men struggled on the floor both trying to reach their weapons, Gray began to shout for the guards, Thomas knew that in a matter of seconds the room would be swarming with SS guards and there would be no chance of escape.

Simon was just inside the craft watching the struggle when Gray had started yelling for the guards, a few seconds later the guards that had been stationed just outside the door came rushing in, there were four of them with automatic weapons. Simon slid a bit deeper into the craft and aimed the watch at Gray.

There was only one choice: he couldn't leave Thomas to die. As the guards closed in, Simon scanned the craft's walls for a lever or button to seal the door. He'd be safe inside–if only he could read the strange writing, it was identical to what Thomas had shown him from the note pilfered at Beck's home. Time ran out. Simon pressed the knob atop his watch. A blinding white flash erupted, striking Gray's left shoulder and sending him sprawling.

Thomas reacted instantly. He seized his weapon and fired at the stunned guards. Two dropped where they stood; the other pair raised their rifles, only to be hurled down by a second burst of white light from Simon's watch. One fallen rifle discharged as it clattered against the floor, spitting out errant rounds.

“Run for the tunnel–now!” Thomas shouted, dashing toward the exit.

“Wait! I still need to set the bomb's timer!” Simon called, racing back to the device. “Hurry, Simon! They've heard the shooting–more will be on us soon.”

“I'm almost done–go ahead! I'll catch up!” Simon replied, hands flying over the bomb's controls.

Thomas hesitated; Simon had saved his life twice in seconds, he couldn't leave him. At that moment, the doors where the guards had entered burst open again and five more SS troopers stormed in, weapons blazing. Thomas unleashed another beam of blue light into their midst, stole a glance at the craft, then bolted for the tunnel–leaving Simon behind.

Inside, Simon heard the echo of gunfire and saw the flash of Thomas's weapon. Trapped once more, he peered out to find SS guards with automatic rifles converging just beyond the doorway. Three broke off and chased Thomas into the tunnel; a fourth stayed behind to tend to Beck, Gray, and the others who had fallen.

Simon crouched inside the alien vessel, heart hammering against his ribs. His fingers hovered over the incomprehensible symbols etched into what appeared to be a control panel. Each marking might seal the door–or trigger something far worse. Outside, boots pounded across concrete as more guards converged on the building. Time was running out.

Taking a deep breath, Simon began pressing buttons at random, praying for a miracle. His gaze settled on a single black leather chair positioned in the center of the craft, its wide armrests gleaming under the dim light. Before it stood a console with twin levers flanking a central joystick. With nowhere else to turn, Simon lowered himself into the seat. The craft hummed to life instantly–panels illuminating in sequence as the control board slid toward him. The door sealed with a pneumatic hiss.

Outside, gunfire erupted as bullets ricocheted harmlessly off the hull. Simon exhaled slowly. He was safe for now, but trapped in a vessel he couldn't operate, surrounded by enemies who wouldn't leave until they had him.

Thomas reached the tunnel, dispatching the three pursuing guards before arriving at the small red brick entrance they'd used earlier that night. Standing at the threshold, he knew the entire town would soon be on high alert. His chances of escape seemed slim until an idea struck him.

Returning to the fallen guards, Thomas located one roughly his size and donned the man's uniform. With luck, the chaos would provide enough cover for him to slip away unnoticed. Though Simon weighed heavily on his mind, Thomas couldn't risk returning. He could only hope his companion would escape and make it to their predetermined rendezvous point.

Meanwhile, Simon sat inside the alien craft, desperately seeking a way out. He grasped the center control stick and tentatively moved it rightward. The craft responded, shifting slightly in that direction. A surge of hope rushed through him–this could be his escape route if only he could see where he was going. After pressing several buttons at random, a screen descended before him, displaying a crystal-clear view of the exterior. Simon marveled at the image quality, so vivid it was like gazing through a window with his own eyes.

Through the viewscreen, Simon watched the guards circling the craft, their faces etched with the same wonder that had seized him earlier. Across the room, Beck was regaining consciousness, a guard helping him to his feet. Simon's pulse quickened–Beck would know how to breach the vessel. Gripping the control stick, Simon yanked it rightward. The craft pivoted smoothly in response, the screen's image shifting to reveal his new heading. As he maintained pressure on the lever, the massive wall of the building filled the display. It was now or never.

Simon slammed the stick forward. The craft lurched, accelerating toward the barrier. He squeezed his eyes shut as the red brick wall rushed towards him. Would the vessel punch through? Shatter on impact? Or worse–detonate in a blinding fireball?

Thomas marched through the town square, the stolen SS uniform's wool collar scratching his neck. The disguise worked perfectly–amid the wailing sirens and shouted German commands, he was just another black-uniformed figure in the chaos. He had almost reached the shadowed archway leading to the train station when the night split apart behind him. The sound hit like artillery fire–a thunderous crack followed by the shriek of twisting metal and crumbling masonry.

Thomas spun around as the alien craft erupted through the brick wall, trailing dust and debris in its wake. The vessel gleamed silver-blue under the moonlight, its smooth hull unmarked despite the violence of its emergence. It hovered momentarily, then lurched forward, its underside reflecting eerily in the cobblestones below. Thomas stood transfixed as it passed directly overhead, close enough that he felt the strange electric hum prickling across his scalp. Inside the craft, Simon's white-knuckled grip relaxed slightly. The impact he'd braced for had felt like nothing more than bumping into a paper screen. He pulled back on the control lever, bringing the vessel to a perfect stop above the town square.

Through the crystalline viewscreen, he watched the upturned faces of townspeople and soldiers alike, their expressions shifting from confusion to terror. Flashlight beams crisscrossed the craft's underbelly while officers gestured wildly, their shouted commands lost in the craft's perfect silence.

When the craft broke through the outer wall of the large red brick building it collapsed in on itself crashing down upon Beck, Gray and the guards inside. Thomas looked back at the fallen building, nothing could survive that he thought silently to himself. His attention was directed back to the hovering craft, he didn't know how Simon had figured out how to fly the thing, he was looking at the craft when it started spinning rapidly counter clockwise, gaining speed as it spun and then suddenly a bright blue flash of light enveloped the craft and then it was gone, nothing left but silence.

Thomas stood there staring at the spot where the craft had been, not sure what had just happened. The craft was gone, nothing left behind, people were starting to fill the square, and Thomas knew he had to leave now so he turned and went into the night.

Chapter 38

Bangor, Maine
January 2001

"So what you are saying is that you are some sort of agent from another world and you have been here since the 1800's?" Kevin asked Thomas as they sat at the breakfast table.

"You could say that," Thomas nodded as he sipped his warm coffee.

"Do you have any special powers?" Kevin asked still peppering Thomas with questions.

"No, not really, the only real difference between you and I is that I age much slower than you do, about one year for every seventy or so of yours," Thomas said.

"Let him come up for air and eat his breakfast," Jack said as he interrupted Kevin's questioning.

"There will be plenty of time for questions later; right now, we need to get a plan together to go get that gold watch back that Beck and his men took the other night," Jack said as he downed a big bite of his mother's pancakes.

Over breakfast Jack, Kevin, Thomas and Jacks father George talked about what they needed to do. Jack's father would be the researcher; he would be the one who would do the research needed to find possible locations of the other gold watches and with the help of Kevin and his crafty computer programs he would have access to any database in the world. Kevin would go along with Jack and Thomas in search of the watches. Their first stop would be to recover the watch that Beck and his helper had taken from the museum a few nights back and that meant their first stop would be Washington D.C.

Thomas suspected that Beck and the other Deceivers would already be making plans to use the watch in another effort to take over the world.

"So what does this thing do, is it some kind of phone?" Kevin asked as he looked at the small black case sitting on the table next to Thomas.

"It does many different things," Thomas said as he thought to himself how he was really starting to like Kevin.

“Can I check it out?” Kevin asked as he looked at it more intently.

“You will not be able to use it; it is designed only to work if in the possession of the one it was assigned to,” said Thomas as he handed it over to Kevin and took a final bite of pancakes.

“You mean it knows who the user is?” Kevin said as he held the small black case in his hands.

“Yes, something like that,” Thomas said amused at Kevin’s interest.

Kevin walked off into the other room with the black case, Thomas and Jack went back to making their plans on how they were going to get the watch back. It would be very dangerous, and Thomas wanted to make sure that he was very clear about what they were about to walk into.

“Hey, this thing is neat,” Kevin said as he came back into the kitchen holding the small black case with its screen fully lit up.

Thomas was surprised when he saw the screen illuminated, “How did you do that?” he asked.

“It wasn’t too hard, once I figured out what the trigger was that recognized the user,” Kevin said as he began to move his finger around the screen. “I love the interface, who would have ever thought you could make a touch screen this small? I think that we all should have one of these,” added Kevin. “There is no way we can duplicate the technology and as I said, there is more to that than you know,” Thomas said as he reached out to take the black case back.

Kevin's eyes lit up as his finger traced patterns on the screen. "Does this gadget have a name?"

"No," Thomas replied, extending his hand. "Now if you'll just–"

A blinding beam erupted from the device, striking the far wall with a crack like thunder. The smell of scorched plaster filled the kitchen.

Kevin froze, mouth agape. "Holy–"

"I warned you, it was more than it seemed," Thomas said firmly, plucking the case from Kevin's stunned fingers.

"Mrs. Douglas, I'm so sorry about your wall," Kevin stammered, staring at the smoking, fist-sized crater in the plaster.

Jack rushed over to examine the damage. "Everyone okay?" He turned to Thomas, eyes wide. "What exactly did it just do?"

"It's primarily a weapon, though it serves many purposes," Thomas admitted, his tone suggesting he'd finally decided to reveal the whole truth.

Kevin's scientific curiosity quickly overcame his shock. "We could really use that kind of firepower. Couldn't we all benefit from having one?"

Thomas shook his head. "This technology can't be reproduced with Earth's resources."

"Let me study it more closely," Kevin persisted. "Maybe I could adapt some of its features to help our mission."

“It is dangerous as I said, I don’t think it would be a good idea,” Thomas said not wanting to risk Kevin blowing them all up.

“Just show me how I armed the thing so I won’t accidently do it again and then you have nothing to worry about,” Kevin pressed. Thomas looked at Jack and then back at Kevin. “I suppose I can do that, but you must be careful,” Thomas cautioned as he handed the small black case to Kevin.

Kevin took the small case into Jacks fathers’ office and pulled out his laptop and a note pad and began to work on understanding what made the case function.

Jack, Thomas and Jack’s father George all sat back down at the table and worked on finalizing their plan for their trip to Washington D.C. George would search for any information that might give a clue to what the Deceivers might be planning; he also would begin searching for possible locations of the other missing gold watches. The plan was set; they would leave for Washington D.C. on the first flight out in the morning.

Chapter 39

Washington, D.C.
January 2001

Detective Susan Young stared at her phone, Commissioner Black's words still ringing in her ears. "Nothing on those security tapes," he'd said, then casually assigned her to track down the vanished Mr. Grant before hanging up. The lie about the tapes was obvious–but why? And why this sudden interest in Grant? Whatever connected these two men, Black considered it important enough to deceive one of his own detectives.

Finding Grant proved nearly impossible. Susan spent hours chasing dead-end addresses and non-existent phone numbers. His background information dissolved into nothing when scrutinized–exactly like Commissioner Black's history had when she'd investigated him earlier. Both men seemed to exist only in the present moment, their pasts carefully erased.

On a hunch, Susan contacted every airline servicing the D.C. area. Her persistence paid off–a passenger named Grant had flown to Boston the same day her mystery man checked himself out of the hospital. It wasn't much, but in an investigation filled with ghosts and lies, even this thin thread was worth following. But Susan couldn't help but wonder how a man who'd barely been able to speak hours earlier somehow manage to check himself out and catch the first flight to Boston, she needed to find him.

Detective Young's methodical tracking revealed his path: Boston to Portland, Maine, then immediately on to Bangor that same night. Now, according to the flight manifest, he was scheduled to return to D.C. this very morning. He would land at Reagan International within the hour.

Susan grabbed her keys and headed for her car. The ease of tracking him puzzled her. A man truly running would have covered his tracks better. Perhaps he wasn't afraid of his attackers following him–or maybe he didn't know who they were. But that raised another question: why was Commissioner Black so invested in finding him? Something wasn't adding up. She needed to speak with Grant again, face to face, and soon.

Susan pulled into a parking space at Reagan International and checked her watch–twenty minutes until Grant's flight landed, plenty of time to find the gate. While scanning the arrivals board, she couldn't shake the questions circling in her mind. What was she missing? Why was Black so fixated on Grant? And those security tapes–why lie about them?

She pulled out her phone and business card for John Wells, head of security at George Washington Hospital. She called him right after meeting Black, warning him someone might come asking about those tapes.

The phone rang twice. "Wells here," came the booming voice.

"Detective Young, Mr. Wells. Hope I'm not catching you at a bad time?"

"Not at all. What can I do for you?"

"Just wanted to thank you for your discretion about my viewing those tapes."

"Hardly matters now," Wells said. "They showed up right after your call and confiscated everything. Made me swear I hadn't kept copies." His voice lowered. "Don't think they believed me though. My office was ransacked that night, and the next day, my house."

Susan watched travelers hurrying past, her unease growing. "Something serious is happening here. What could possibly be on those tapes?" She thought to herself.

"I appreciate your help. I'll be in touch." Susan ended the call, her suspicions now a certainty.

A crackle over the loudspeaker announced that Flight 94 from Maine was landing and would pull into the gate in a few minutes. Susan's pulse quickened. She couldn't wait to question Mr. Grant–but she wasn't ready to tell Commissioner Black she'd already located him, not until she learned why he'd lied about his interest in Thomas Grant.

Pushing through the crowd of arriving passengers, Susan almost passed him by–Thomas blended so perfectly into the milling throng. She finally spotted him flanked by two companions, who were animatedly discussing something they needed to find.

"Mr. Grant," Susan said, touching Thomas's elbow as she came alongside him.

He turned, startled to see Detective Susan Young. "Detective Young! What a surprise."

"I wondered if we could talk," she said, nodding toward a nearby bench. Thomas exchanged glances with the two others, then led her to a vacant seat.

Kevin, one of the men, raised an eyebrow. "And who might this be?" He studied the striking woman beside Thomas.

"Detective Susan Young," she replied, extending her hand with a polite smile.

"These are my friends Kevin and Jack," Thomas said quickly, before Kevin could speak.

"Pleased to meet you," Jack muttered with a brief nod. Thomas turned back to Susan. "Are you traveling?" "I'm here to talk," she said. "You left the hospital so suddenly, I never got to finish my questions about your case. How are you feeling? The last time I saw you, you didn't seem on your feet."

"Much better, thank you, Detective," Thomas replied, shifting from one foot to the other. "I wasn't aware you needed more information."

"I called the number and address on your file, but neither was valid," Susan said, holding his gaze. "Then I discovered you were arriving on a flight from Maine."

Thomas forced a small, uneasy smile. "There must've been some kind of mix-up."

Jack and Kevin retreated a few steps, hovering near a bank of payphones. Kevin drummed his fingers against his thigh while Jack's eyes darted between Thomas and the detective–a tall woman with copper-brown hair pulled back in a severe bun that emphasized her sharp cheekbones.

"Mr. Grant, I know you are not telling me the truth," Detective Young said, her voice cool as polished steel. Her badge glinted under the harsh fluorescent lights of the terminal.

"Detective, I am–" Thomas's weathered face tightened, the lines around his mouth deepening.

"Mr. Grant," she interrupted, leaning forward until he could smell her mint-laced breath, "Why don't you tell me about the gold watch and why my police commissioner is so interested in your case?"

The words hit Thomas like ice water. His pupils contracted to pinpoints. The detective's knowledge of the watch and mention of the commissioner transported him instantly back to the museum steps–Beck's predatory smile, the glint of light on his companion's mirrored sunglasses. The Deceivers knew. They were coming.

"Detective, I do not understand what you are asking me," Thomas replied, his voice steady despite the tremor in his left hand. He scanned the bustling terminal, his gaze skipping over luggage carts and hurried travelers.

He missed the two men in charcoal suits at the coffee kiosk across the concourse, one stirring his espresso with mechanical precision, the other's pale eyes fixed unblinkingly on Thomas over the rim of his cup.

Chapter 40

Washington, D.C.
January 2001

Gray and his younger partner waited at the coffee-shop counter. A few yards away, Thomas Grant stood talking with Detective Susan Young. It had been Beck's idea to send Gray and Jason Wright–an eager young Deceiver anxious to prove himself–to tail the detective. Beck suspected that Detective Young would soon encounter Mr. Grant, and he wasn't convinced she'd willingly lead Grant back to them, especially after she'd lied to Black about the security tapes.

"Mr. Grant, I don't know what you're hiding, but I will find out," Young said. "If I were you, I wouldn't plan on leaving town anytime soon."

"I assure you, Detective, I've done nothing wrong."

"Then give me a real phone number. Not another phony."

"I don't have one," Grant replied. "I travel constantly and have no permanent line."

"You don't carry a cell phone or pager?"

"No, I don't," Thomas said, shaking his head. "That black case wasn't a phone either."

Young's eyes narrowed. "What was it?"

"A tape recorder," he answered–technically not a complete lie, though the device wasn't exactly a recorder.

Detective Young held his gaze. Something about him felt honest; she couldn't shake the sense that he was trying to protect her rather than deceive her. Susan prided herself on reading people, and her gut told her Thomas Grant was on the level.

Before she could press further, a voice interrupted. "Detective, I'll give you my cell number," Kevin said, stepping forward. "Thomas here–he doesn't even know how to work one. If you need him, just call me." He pressed a small slip of paper into Susan's hand.

"Thank you," she said, tucking the note into her pocket.

"No problem. If you need anything at all, just call. We're in town a few days," Kevin added, delivering the line with a playful smile.

"Okay, that's enough flirting–let's go before the detective draws her gun on you," Jack said, tugging Kevin away.

Thomas, Jack, and Kevin left Detective Young behind and hurried toward the exit. While they were eager to begin their search for the gold watch, Thomas harbored reservations about another confrontation with Beck and his Deceivers. Though he feared his luck might not hold a second time, having Jack and Kevin beside him provided some comfort.

As they approached the line of waiting taxis, they failed to notice two men trailing several paces behind them.

"Where to?" asked the driver in a thick foreign accent.

"The Washington Monument," Jack replied without hesitation.

Thomas studied the driver's reflection in the rearview mirror. Something about the man triggered an instinctive warning, though Thomas couldn't pinpoint exactly why. "I've finished connecting everything," Kevin announced, handing Jack what appeared to be a hybrid between a phone and calculator. "Just press the person's number, and you'll have a direct line between devices."

Jack examined the gadget with confusion. "What exactly is this?"

"Custom communicators," Kevin explained. "They work on a secure frequency and can access Thomas's information-gathering system. We'll need to recharge them every few days–I'm not sure what power source Thomas uses for his."

Jack turned the device over in his hands, impressed by Kevin's ingenuity in creating something so sophisticated in such a short time. His curiosity was definitely piqued.

"Nice work," he said, slipping the device into his jacket pocket.

Just a few cars back following the taxi was Gray, the plan had been set and in just a few moments all three would be dead and with any luck another of the gold pocket watches would be found.

The cab turned off the main road and headed down a smaller side street among old warehouse type buildings. Thomas now knew that there was something wrong and that they were in danger, he gave a quick glance over his shoulder and saw the large black vehicle following behind the cab, they had been found by the Deceivers.

Thomas reached into his pocket and pulled his small black case; he quickly sent a message to Jack's communicator. THE DECEIVERS HAVE US! was all the message said. A few moments passed and Jack felt a slight vibration in his pocket, he reached in and pulled the gizmo out and looked at the screen, a chill ran down his spine as he read over the words for a second time. He slipped the gizmo back into his pocket and gave a quick glance at Thomas as if nothing were out of the ordinary.

The car slowed and turned into a smaller side street and then turned into an open gate at the side of a large vacant looking building. "This doesn't look like the way to the Washington Monument," Jack said to the driver.

The driver looked into his rearview mirror at the three men and gave a sly grin and said nothing as the car pulled into the building and came to a stop.

It was dark inside the large empty building, but Jack could make out three figures standing in the shadows, the cab driver spun around in his seat with a strange looking weapon pointed at them.

"Get out of the car now!" The driver ordered speaking in a normal American accent.

Kevin's eyes widened as realization struck. "What's happening here?"

"Out of the vehicle now," the driver commanded, his voice hardening to steel, "unless you prefer to die where you sit."

They slipped out of the taxi and huddled beside it in the gloom. Jack counted four silhouettes lurking in the darkness–the three original figures plus the driver from the car that had tailed them.

"Why target us?" Jack asked, in a tone that did not give a hint of any fear, his voice steady with defiance.

A man emerged from the shadows; his finger aimed at Thomas like a weapon. "Perhaps your companion can enlighten you." His lips curled into a knowing smile. "You're well aware of what we seek, aren't you, Mr. Grant?"

Thomas met Beck's gaze without flinching. "I know what you're after, but you won't get it from me."

Beck circled Thomas like a predator, his footsteps echoing in the warehouse. "The last of the Protectors, standing right before me. We've hunted your kind across this miserable rock for centuries." His voice dropped to a whisper. "And your leader–he can't hide forever." Jack's eyes darted to Thomas. Leader? Thomas had never mentioned any leader.

"Deny it all you want," Beck continued, leaning in close enough that Thomas could smell his breath. "Your precious leader is on Earth, and his days are numbered."

Beck's smile vanished. "The watch. Where is it?" His eyes narrowed to dark slits, decades of hatred visible in their depths.

The strike came without warning–Beck's open palm connecting with Thomas's cheek with a crack that echoed through the warehouse. Thomas staggered but remained standing.

"Pathetic," Beck hissed, shaking out his hand. "Did you honestly believe you could save these worthless humans from us?"

Blood trickled from the corner of Thomas's mouth, but he remained silent. The certainty of his own death weighed on him–as did the knowledge that Beck would claim another watch. At least their leader's location would remain secret; that thought alone gave him some comfort. Yet watching Jack and Kevin standing there, marked for death, brought back the raw anguish of witnessing Simon's murder all those years ago.

Detective Young crouched in the shadows of the warehouse, her hand hovering near her holster. She'd tailed the cab on instinct, unconvinced by Thomas's evasive answers. The voices echoing through the cavernous space confirmed her suspicions–this was no friendly meeting.

Through the gloom, she identified Beck from the security footage–the same man who'd been with Commissioner Black. Speaking of whom, there stood the Commissioner himself alongside Senator Buckley. Two other figures remained obscured in the darkness, their faces turned away.

Her mind raced through options. Intervention meant risking four lives instead of three, but standing by wasn't an option. What business did a Police Commissioner and a US Senator have with these armed thugs? "Surprised to see me again?" Beck's voice carried across the warehouse as he circled Thomas like a shark. "And who might your companions be?"

Jack's voice cut through the tension. "Someone who doesn't answer to you."

Beck's hand whipped toward Jack's face, but Jack's reflexes proved faster. His fingers locked around Beck's wrist, stopping the blow mid-strike.

"Bad move," Jack said, his voice dangerously calm.

"Release him," commanded a man holding what looked like no ordinary weapon against Kevin's temple, "unless you want to watch your friend die."

Jack unclenched his fingers. Beck retreated, massaging his wrist with a scowl.

"Seems we have a fighter who doesn't grasp his predicament," Beck said, exchanging glances with his accomplices.

“I am tired of wasting time, where is the watch? I will count to three and then I will kill your young friend here,” Beck said as Gray grabbed Kevin and tossed him to the ground with the weapon pointed at his head.

“I can assure you he won’t miss as he did with you the other night.”

“One, two...”

Beck's mouth opened to say "three" when a deafening crack split the air. A crimson flash illuminated Gray's face as he staggered backward, a dark stain blooming across his chest before he crumpled to the concrete.

In the chaos that followed, Jack vaulted over Kevin's huddled form, executed a backward roll, and snatched Gray's fallen weapon.

Across the warehouse, Thomas hurled himself at Beck. The two men crashed to the floor, trading blows in a desperate struggle. As Senator Buckley and Commissioner Black lunged toward the scuffle, a commanding voice rang out from the shadows.

"Freeze! Nobody move!" Detective Young stepped into view; her service weapon trained on the officials.

The Commissioner's jaw slackened. "Detective Young? What are you doing here?"

"Following what I thought were three suspects," she replied, her aim unwavering. "Instead, I find two of the city's most respected officials about to execute unarmed civilians."

"These men are dangerous criminals," Black insisted, his voice strained. "They stole valuable property–"

"Enough!" The Senator's voice cut through the warehouse like a blade. "You've compromised everything with your incompetence, Commissioner. I should never have trusted you with this operation."

The senator reached into his pocket and pulled a weapon and began to shoot at the detective. Jack pointed and pulled the trigger on his weapon and fired a blue blast of light from it, but his aim was off. It hit the Commissioner and threw him into the Senator just as he pulled his trigger; the blue light flashed from his weapon and hit the ceiling, blowing a hole clear through exposing the sky.

The Commissioner lay on the floor, dead along with Gray who had been shot through the heart by the detective.

They were in a standoff, the Senator had his weapon pointed at Kevin and Jack had his pointed at Jason, while Thomas held Beck to the floor and Detective Young had her gun pointed directly at the Senator.

“Here is what is going to happen, you will let Beck up and we are going to walk out of here or your friend here dies, your choice detective,” the Senator said as he held his weapon pointed at Kevin.

“If you shoot him, I shoot you and you die right here along with him,” Detective Young snapped back trying to buy some time to figure out what her next move should be.

“It’s ok detective, I will let him up,” Thomas said as he lessened his grip on Beck who immediately struggled to his feet and stood next to the Senator.

“I knew they would let me go, they don’t have the guts for this,” Beck said as he wiped blood from his mouth with his coat sleeve.

Thomas stood next to the detective and moved his hand into his pocket and placed it on the small black case and armed it.

“Come on Senator, let’s get out of here,” Beck said as he took a step back.

“No, we came for the watch and that’s what we’re going to get before we go,” the Senator said as he held his gun on Kevin.

“Give it up or he is dead and I won’t count to three.”

“Ok, just don’t shoot; I have it here in my pocket,” Thomas said as a brilliant blue flash shot from his pocket and hit the senator squarely on the chest and sent him hurling back on to the floor.

In the same instant Jason lunged at Jack who shot him in the stomach, sending him falling dead to the floor.

During the commotion Beck turned and ran into the dark of the building and disappeared, Jack gave chase but soon lost Beck and returned to the others.

Kevin's hands wouldn't stop shaking. "What the hell just happened?"

Jack crossed to his friend, stepping around the bodies. "You alright?"

"Ask me when my pulse gets below two hundred." Kevin's laugh came out more like a gasp. Detective Young holstered her weapon and knelt beside the Senator, pressing two fingers against his neck. She shook her head. "Nothing." Her eyes fixed on Thomas. "So, what makes this watch worth killing a U.S. Senator over?"

Thomas exchanged glances with Jack and Kevin. "It's complicated. And lengthy."

"Well, I've got four corpses on my hands," Young said, gesturing around the warehouse. "Two of them high-profile. I need answers before I call this in."

Kevin let out a hollow laugh. "Lady, you have no idea how deep this rabbit hole goes."

"Try me," Young said, her expression hardening. "Because right now, I'm standing in a warehouse with four dead men, including a Police Commissioner and a Senator. So, start talking."

Jack tucked Gray's alien weapon into his jacket pocket, the metal still warm against his side. "We need to move," he said, glancing at the warehouse's rusted skylights. "Beck knows every cop in the city. This place will be crawling with his people in minutes."

He handed the Senator's weapon to Kevin, who accepted it with trembling fingers, the blue-tinged barrel reflecting in his wide eyes.

Young's unmarked Crown Victoria sliced through the downpour, hydroplaning around corners as they escaped the warehouse district. Hours later, under the buzzing fluorescents of her kitchen–surrounded by framed commendations and cardboard containers crusted with leftover lo Mein–Thomas laid bare the impossible truth. She listened, her expression transforming from skeptical squint to widened disbelief to the tight-jawed resignation of someone whose world had just imploded.

When the first gray light filtered through her blinds, Young pushed back from the table and met their eyes. "So, how do we track down Beck?"

With those seven words, she became the fifth member of The Five, now facing a war against an enemy older than human civilization.

ABOUT THE AUTHOR

DUSTIN MCCLAIN was born in Oregon and now lives in Indiana with his wife Susan. He enjoys spending time with his daughter Lucy, reading history and creating entertaining stories of which he is currently in the middle of writing his second book.

PG

PAPER AND GLUE BOOKS

Visit our website for more titles by this author
paperandgluebooks.com

www.ingramcontent.com/pod-product-compliance
Lightning Source LLC
LaVergne TN
LVHW010946110826
845149LV00015B/3233

* 9 7 9 8 9 9 3 9 9 7 0 2 5 *